RENDEZVOUS IN RUSSIA

A LAURA MARLIN MYSTERY
RENDEZVOUS IN RUSSIA

Lauren St John

Illustrated by David Dean

Orion
Children's Books

First published in Great Britain in 2013
by Orion Children's Books
This paperback edition first published in Great Britain in 2014
by Orion Children's Books
a division of the Orion Publishing Group Ltd
Orion House
5 Upper St Martin's Lane
London WC2H 9EA
An Hachette UK Company

3 5 7 9 10 8 6 4 2

A catalogue record for this book
is available from the British Library

ISBN 978 1 4440 0945 3

www.laurenstjohn.com

www.orionbooks.co.uk

*For my mother, who gave me three of the greatest gifts
you could give any child: a love of reading and travelling,
and a belief in the power of dreams*

'CUT!' YELLED THE director. 'Cut, cut, cut!'

He was a gaunt man with a receding hairline and small, round glasses that perched high on the bridge of his beaked nose, giving him the air of a worried crow. Leaning into the sea wind, his face turning fire-engine red, he bore down on the hapless dog handler cowering on the edge of the film set. Actors and assorted crew scurried from his path.

'You imbecile! You absolute dunce! Call yourself an animal trainer? You couldn't teach a mouse to eat cheese. You couldn't teach a horse to graze grass. You couldn't teach a bird to fly, or a cheetah to chase antelope, or a fish to swim. What did I tell you yesterday, Otto? For the fiftieth time, I instructed you to find me a dog I would love, a dog with attitude, a dog that will have cinema audiences across the world cheering one moment and reaching for the tissues the next. And what do you do? You produce a greyhound with the attention span of a goldfish. We've also had an obese golden retriever too lazy to do a single trick, yet with all the energy in the world when it came to gobbling three trays of smoked salmon sandwiches from the catering unit. We've had a border collie with rickets, a deranged spaniel and a bull terrier that almost amputated the hand of my supporting actress. If she hadn't been an animal lover, the lawsuit would have bankrupted the studio.'

He shook his fist. 'One more chance, my friend. If the next mutt you bring me isn't capable of winning an Oscar, you're fired.'

A crowd had gathered behind the ropes keeping onlookers from wandering on to the set. The woman beside Laura rolled her eyes. 'Oh dear. If the next scene goes wrong, I'm afraid that Brett will spontaneously combust. I don't suppose you'd consider volunteering your dog for the role? He's an extraordinary looking animal. A bit like a wolf, only kinder. Anyone would fall in love with him.'

Laura glowed with pride. She hugged Skye, her three-legged Siberian husky, and his tail thumped ecstatically. 'You'd be surprised. I think he's the most amazing dog on the planet, but—'

'And so do I,' put in Tariq, her best friend.

'But what?' asked the woman, who was dressed simply in jeans and a pale blue shirt but had the poise and photogenic features of an actress.

'Well, I think Skye is perfect, but not everyone feels the same way,' Laura said. 'Your director sounds very fussy. If he can't cope with a fat retriever, I doubt he'd want a husky with a missing leg.'

The woman laughed. 'Oh, don't pay any attention to Brett. He's all bluster. Beneath it, he's a bit of a geek. And he's super talented – one of the hottest movie-makers in Hollywood. There's a lot of excitement about our film. We've only been shooting for a week and already there's talk of awards.'

'What's the title of your movie?' asked Tariq. He and Laura had been overjoyed to discover, on the first day of the summer holidays, that a film set had mushroomed overnight on the outskirts of St Ives, their seaside home town. As a special treat, they'd begun the morning with breakfast at the Sunny Side Up cafe, but as soon as they'd swallowed the last delicious bite they'd begged permission from Laura's uncle to go out onto the cliffs and watch the filming.

'No running off to Hollywood now,' Calvin Redfern joked as they'd left.

'The title of our film is *The Aristocratic Thief*,' the woman told them. 'It's set in the nineteenth century and is about a wealthy man, renowned and respected in the highest circles in the land, who steals a priceless painting from the Hermitage Museum in St Petersburg, Russia. That's where we're filming next.'

'If it's set in Russia, what are you doing in Cornwall?' Laura wanted to know.

'We're shooting the English bit of the movie. In the story, the child heroine of the film is an orphan who comes from a beautiful seaside town. She has a dog she adores. This pet plays a vital role in the film, which is why it's a disaster that we're having so much difficulty finding the right one.'

She smiled. 'I haven't introduced myself. I'm Kay Allbright.'

Laura shook her hand. 'I'm Laura Marlin and this is my best friend, Tariq, and my husky, Skye. Do you mind me asking if you're an actress?'

'Was. A long time ago. Now I have the job of my dreams. I'm a screenwriter. I get to research and write the film itself. It's challenging and frequently frustrating, but I'm passionate about it.'

Skye stiffened. His blue eyes were locked on the dog handler, who was carrying a yapping Pomeranian onto the set. Laura took a firm grip on his collar. 'Behave yourself, Skye,' she scolded. 'You've already had breakfast.'

Beyond the cameras was an encampment of tents and caravans, plus a catering trailer with a red and white striped awning. The door of the largest caravan opened and out came a girl of about twelve or thirteen with long flaxen hair, wearing a ragged dress of white muslin. Her striking prettiness was marred by a bored scowl. Fortunately for the dog handler, it vanished as soon as she saw the Pomeranian.

'Oh he's so cute!' she cried in an American accent. 'What's his name?'

The man looked relieved. 'Her name is Britney. She's quite the little actress. Loves attention. I should have used her from the start. You even have the same hair colour.'

'That's Ana María Tyler, who plays the orphan heroine of the story,' Kay whispered to Laura and Tariq. 'She's barely in her teens and she already has five movies under her belt.' She added under her breath: 'And an attitude to match.'

The director strode onto the set. 'Is this the best that you could come up with, Otto – a Pomeranian? Give me strength. How many times do you want me to explain that we need a dog capable of saving a young girl's life, or stopping an arch villain? This one couldn't scare a canary.'

Ana María pouted and clutched Britney to her chest. 'Yes, but she is a dog that audiences will go gooey over and you said that's important too.'

'True,' acknowledged Brett. 'Very true. Okay, we'll give Miss Britney a shot. Let go of her so that Otto can put her on her marker. Crew, take up your stations. Ready, Ana María? Action!'

The cameras rolled. As Laura and Tariq leaned forward eagerly, a low growl rumbled in Skye's throat. Laura soothed him with one hand and took a firmer grip on his collar with the other. He seemed to think that Britney would make a yummy mid-morning snack.

Ana María strolled along the cliff in the sunshine, admiring the view over the shining sea. The Pomeranian was with Otto, out of sight. Ana María bent down to pick wild flowers from the waving grass. One, a poppy, was slightly out of reach. She leaned closer to the edge and stretched for it.

Laura knew she was only acting but it was nerve-wracking to watch.

As Ana María's fingers closed around the poppy, there was a horrible cracking sound. The section of cliff on which she was kneeling suddenly disintegrated, catapulting her, screaming, over the edge.

Laura gave an involuntary shriek.

'Don't worry,' whispered Kay. 'It's all part of the show. She's landed on a specially constructed ledge and is quite safe. There's also a net beneath should anything go wrong.'

'I hope they've secured them well,' Tariq said worriedly. 'If she did fall, she'd almost certainly be killed. If she wasn't crushed on the rocks, she'd be drowned. The currents around here are incredibly strong.'

Laura couldn't repress a shudder. Tariq was speaking from experience. Barely six months earlier, he and Laura had come close to dying at Dead Man's Cove, only a stone's throw from where they were standing. Even now she could feel the power of the sea as it had sucked at her, trying to drag her into its freezing black depths.

Ana María was clinging to the rocky ledge by her fingers. 'Help!' she screamed. 'Help!'

Britney the Pomeranian went tearing across the cliff top, yapping for all she was worth. Her role was to run to Ana María's aid, realise there was a problem, and race away to get help. At least, that was the plan.

Unfortunately, nobody had communicated that to Skye. The husky took one look at Britney bounding like a bunny through the long grass, wrenched out of Laura's grasp and tore after her.

Laura clapped her hands to her mouth in horror. She dared not call him while the cameras were rolling, but how else was she to stop him? Kay and Tariq were also frozen to the spot. All they could do was watch the disaster unfold.

As Britney neared the screaming actress, some sixth sense warned her of approaching danger. She glanced over her shoulder and let out an audible squeak when she saw the husky bearing down on her. Realising that escape was impossible, she chose to leap over the cliff, landing on the ledge that Ana María was holding onto.

'Ouch!' screeched Ana María as Britney's claws dug into her hand. She let go. That shouldn't have mattered because she was standing on a wide wooden platform which had been cleverly painted to blend in with the rocks and was invisible to the cameras. Unfortunately, the jolt to the plank caused the fastenings that secured it to the rock to loosen. It only slipped a couple of millimetres, but it was enough to make Ana María lose her balance and come close to falling. This time, her blood-curdling scream had nothing to do with acting.

'CUT!' yelled the director, but no one appeared to be listening.

'Skye!' yelled Laura. 'Skye!'

She ducked under the ropes and sprinted to the edge of the cliff, followed by Tariq and Kay. Chaos broke out on the set.

'Do something!' Brett Avery shouted at the stunt

coordinator. 'What do you think I pay you for? Go down and get her. Call the coastguard, call the fire brigade, call the Queen if you have to, just get my star back on solid ground.'

Cautiously, he leaned over the cliff. 'Ana María, honey, whatever you do, don't look down.'

Ana María immediately glanced at the sea churning far below and screamed even louder. The Pomeranian whimpered and whined.

The stunt expert was trying to wriggle into a climbing harness while yelling at his assistant to get a rope that the actress could hold on to until he reached her. Ana María's mother, who'd appeared out of nowhere, added to the din by crying hysterically and threatening to sue.

The weight of people gathered on the clifftop caused a further loosening of the unstable edge. Pellets of gravel rained down on Ana María and the Pomeranian. Britney yapped madly. Ana María sobbed and shook.

'What the devil's taking so long?' yelled the director, but the stunt coordinator didn't answer. He was staring at his climbing harness in confusion. 'I don't understand,' he mumbled. 'I don't understand.'

'Something is wrong,' Tariq whispered to Laura as the adults began to argue. 'He looks as if he's lost something.'

Ana María gave a screech that could have shattered a pane of glass. The wind was picking up and threatening to suck her off the cliff.

The stunt assistant came racing up with a spare rope. 'Grab this and hang on tight,' he called down to Ana María. 'Try to stay calm. A lifeboat is on its way and there is a safety net below so you're not in any real danger.'

The words had barely left his mouth when the catastrophe happened. A gust of wind launched Britney into space. Ana María, who was clinging desperately to the rope at the time, was unaware that the Pomeranian had fallen until Britney's furry body flew past her. The little dog hit the water and flailed briefly before disappearing beneath the waves. For an already petrified Ana María, the shock was so great that her legs crumpled beneath her. She swung out over the void, past the safety net.

The stunt coordinator was frantic. 'Hang on tight, Ana María,' he yelled as the actress twirled on the end of the rope, bouncing periodically off the cliff face. 'We're going to pull you up. Whatever you do, don't let go.'

But try as she might, Ana María didn't have the strength to obey. At the first tug of the rope, her hands slipped and she plummeted downwards. She hit the boiling surf and disappeared.

'Now that,' Kay said, 'was not in the script.'

ANA MARÍA'S MOTHER, who was Colombian and quite excitable at the best of times, fainted. The director dropped to his knees and appeared to be praying. Otto, the animal handler, was so distressed that he plucked out at least half of his remaining twenty-six strands of hair.

With the humans going into meltdown, it was perhaps not surprising that the husky was the first to recover. Before Laura could take in what was happening, Skye had twisted from her grasp, taken three rapid strides and leapt off the cliff.

'No, Skye!' she shouted, but it was too late. A plume of spray kicked up and then the ocean swallowed him whole, just as it had Ana María and the Pomeranian.

'Skye!' screamed Laura at the same time as dozens of people started yelling for Ana María and one lone voice for Britney. 'Skye! Somebody call the lifeguard. I have to get down there. I have to save him.'

'I think it's a bit late for that, kid,' the production manager, Jeffrey, announced cruelly. 'Your pet will be fish food by the time we've rescued Ana María. I'm sorry, but that's the way it is.'

Tariq was a mild-mannered boy but he gave the man the most murderous glare he could manage. 'Don't pay any attention to him, Laura,' he said. 'Skye is the smartest dog in the world. He wouldn't have jumped if he didn't think he'd make it.'

Kay let out a cry of disbelief. 'Laura, look!'

A hundred metres below them, Skye had surfaced, swimming strongly. He carried a piece of white cloth in his mouth. There was so much foam that it took a few seconds to make out that it was Ana María's dress and that the barely conscious actress was inside it. Fighting the current, he swam to the rocks and hauled her out of the punishing waves. She lay limply on a boulder as if she was dead.

By now, a crowd numbering well over fifty had gathered on the cliff top. They called encouragingly to Skye as he searched for the drowning Pomeranian. A cheer went up when he plucked the tiny dog from the water and placed her on the rock beside Ana María just as a lifeboat came roaring around the corner.

In a matter of moments, a beefy, white-bearded lifeguard

had Ana María on board and was reviving her with warm blankets and hot, sweet tea. The other, younger lifeguard lifted Skye and the shivering Britney into the boat and they too were wrapped in rugs. As the boat sped away, cheers followed it.

When the crowd had dispersed, Brett Avery said in a shaky voice, 'That husky – where did he come from? Who does he belong to? Will somebody find me his owner and bring them to me RIGHT NOW!'

Laura shrank behind Kay. She had visions of Calvin Redfern, her uncle, who had very little money, being sued for all he owned. They'd lose their home at No.28 Sea View Terrace and have to leave St Ives for somewhere cheaper. Social Services would get involved and drag Laura back to the Sylvan Meadows Home for Girls, the desperately dull orphanage where she'd spent the first eleven years of her life.

'The husky belongs to this young lady here,' Kay said with a smile, pushing Laura forward. 'Wasn't he marvellous? You couldn't make it up. It just goes to show that truth is always stranger than fiction.'

Laura stammered, 'I'm s-sorry Skye messed up your scene and caused such havoc. I was holding him, I promise I was, but you see he's incredibly strong and he saw Britney and . . . Mr Avery, my uncle doesn't have much money so we can't pay you. Maybe I could make it up to you by washing dishes in the catering trailer or something?'

'Pay me? *Pay me?* Kid, I'm the one who should be paying you! Have you any idea what a gift you've just given the studio?' He gave an incredulous laugh. 'You have no idea what I'm talking about, do you? Allow me to explain.'

He gestured to a runner. 'Hey, Chad, do me a favour and bring a couple of catering's best smoothies for our friends.'

Minutes later, Laura and Tariq were sitting in chairs that had in their time seated several legends, chatting to their new friends Kay Allbright and Brett Avery, one of Hollywood's most famous directors. They were sipping mango and coconut smoothies and listening with growing astonishment as Brett talked. It turned out that the cameraman had not stopped filming when the director shouted cut, but had recorded the entire drama.

'Do you know what that means?' Brett demanded. 'It's movie gold. Pure movie gold. With some judicious editing we can use the entire sequence in the film almost as if Kay had written it like that in her screenplay.'

Laura was taken aback. 'But what about Ana María? She could have been killed. Surely she wouldn't want that footage being seen by movie audiences?'

Brett Avery laughed. 'On the contrary, she'll love the publicity. Mark my words, she'll get an Oscar for that performance.'

He put a hand on Laura's arm. 'Which is where you come in, my dear. I must have your hero dog for my movie. Obviously, we couldn't use any of these scenes if we had to find a replacement dog. We could get another husky, but it's unlikely we'd find one with three legs. Besides, this particular dog is the exact dog I've been searching for – a dog with attitude, a dog movie audiences will adore. I want to buy him. How much will you take for him?'

'He's not for sale. I wouldn't part with Skye for all the money in the world.'

Brett said smoothly, 'Of course you wouldn't. But you haven't heard my offer yet. I'm prepared to pay you a thousand pounds for him.'

Laura did her best to hide her shock. 'He's not for sale. Not for any price.'

'Ah, a lady who drives a hard bargain. Five thousand. I'll give you five thousand for him.'

Laura thought of her uncle and what a difference such a sum of money would make to him, but Skye was just as important to her. She shook her head.

The smile left the director's face. 'You obviously love your dog and that's great, but maybe you should think what the money might mean to others. You mentioned that your uncle doesn't have much. I'm prepared to pay you ten thousand pounds for your husky. That's my final offer. It might change your uncle's life.'

'Skye means as much to Laura as her uncle does,' Tariq informed him. 'He's family to her. You don't sell family.'

Brett Avery lost his cool. 'Don't be ridiculous. Animals are not as valuable as people. They can be sweet, yes, but there's no comparison—'

'How about a loan?' Kay interrupted hastily. 'Laura, how would you feel if we borrowed Skye for a couple of weeks of filming in Russia? The studio will pay you and your uncle a handsome fee and you'll have your dog back before you know it. And when *The Aristocratic Thief* opens in cinemas later in the year, you'll be able to boast to your friends that your husky is famous.'

Before Laura could answer, the lifeguard's four-wheel drive came bouncing up the slope, and out stepped Ana María, looking pale, fragile and furious. Her golden hair hung in wet rat's tails.

'We tried to persuade her to go to hospital . . .' the lifeguard told Brett Avery, 'but she insisted on talking to you first.'

The director embraced the sodden actress, then pulled her aside and started talking to her urgently in a voice too low to hear. Laura wondered if he was telling her that the cameraman had recorded every detail of her fall and that she'd doubtless win an Academy Award for it, because her countenance suddenly became sunny. At one point, she turned and stared hard at Laura and Tariq.

Laura was so transfixed by the scene that she was almost bowled over by a damp and sandy Skye, who'd bounded out of the lifeguard's vehicle and raced towards her. She squatted down and he put his left paw on her shoulder and licked her face until she was almost as wet as he was.

'You,' she told him, 'are a total hero. You're the best and bravest dog on earth and I wouldn't part with you for all the money in Hollywood.'

'Watch out, Laura,' Tariq warned. 'Here comes Brett Avery again. Bet he tries to talk you around.'

'He can try. He's not going to get anywhere.'

Brett Avery was all smiles. He pushed his glasses up on his nose. 'Sorry about that, kids. Had to check on our star. What a trooper. A bit bruised and suffering from mild hypothermia, but the show must go on and all that.

Needless to say, she's fallen in love with Skye. You'll be pleased to hear that she's in total agreement with you. Won't hear of the dog being taken away from you, even if it's merely on loan.'

Laura was surprised. 'Really? What about the rescue footage? Will you be able to find another three-legged dog?'

Brett Avery ushered them back to the chairs and called for ice creams. 'Sit down, kids, sit down. What were your names again? Laura Marlin and Tariq Ali. Is that right? Fabulous. Kids, you won't believe this, but even in her traumatised state Ana María noticed something that I should have spotted at once – and in fact would have done had it not been for the crisis.'

'What's that?' asked Tariq, declining the ice cream. His early life as a quarry slave in Bangladesh had made him distrustful of the motives of grown-ups.

'I should have noticed that you're great looking kids. You'd be perfect for my movie. You're an eye-catching pair – Laura with her peachy skin and pale blonde hair, and Tariq with his black hair and caramel skin. Knockout. You're born to be actors.

'We'd have to get permission from your guardians, of course, but how would you feel about starring in my movie, along with Skye? We're wrapping up filming here tomorrow, but at the end of the week we're off to St Petersburg, Russia. We'd need you for about ten days of shooting. We'd pay you handsomely, take care of all your expenses, and you'd essentially have a free holiday in one of the most beautiful cities in the world. Best of all, Skye would be with you. How about it?'

During her years at the orphanage, when it seemed that she'd be stuck in a grim, grey town for ever, Laura had longed for a life of excitement and adventure. More than anything, she'd yearned to travel and see exotic places and few countries seemed more exotic or mysterious than Russia. She glanced quickly at Tariq. Though he was trying hard not to show it, his eyes were alight with excitement. Tariq came from a background even tougher than hers and he too dreamed of seeing the world.

She put an arm around Skye. 'I'd have to ask my uncle's permission and Tariq would need to speak to his foster parents, but I think it's something we'd consider, Mr Avery.'

'Brett. Call me Brett.'

As she made her way back to Sea View Terrace with Skye, Laura was walking on air. For as long as she could remember, she'd dreamed of becoming a detective when she grew up. Unlike many of the girls she knew, she'd never had any desire to become a famous actress. Now the opportunity had unexpectedly landed in her lap. Acting would not have been her first choice of career but, Laura mused as she strolled home, it was always good to have options.

~ 3 ~

'*EXTRAS?* **BRETT AVERY** didn't say anything about us being extras. He told us he was going to make us stars.'

Calvin Redfern smothered a laugh. He filled one mug with hot chocolate and another with black coffee and carried them over to the kitchen table, side-stepping Lottie, his wolfhound, who was basking in the warmth of the Aga. 'Welcome to Hollywood, Laura. Mr Avery tried to tell me the same thing, but I'm afraid I'm rather more cynical. When I pressed him for a job description, he said that while Skye would definitely have a starring role in the movie, you and Tariq would be what he called "background artistes".'

'What does that mean?'

'You'll be crowd scene extras who show up in the credits described as "Girl in Red Hat" or "Boy Pushing Cart." When the film comes out at the cinema, if you blink you'll miss yourselves.'

'Oh,' said Laura, feeling deflated. She'd been looking forward to the expressions on her classmates' faces when she and Tariq returned from the summer holidays as famous film stars. 'Didn't you hear about it?' she'd planned to say airily. 'We were discovered after my husky saved Ana María Tyler's life. The director said we were naturals.'

'Don't look so glum,' said her uncle. 'Since when have you cared about fame and fortune? As far as I know, all you've ever dreamed of is becoming a detective like Matt Walker in those books you love so much. Don't tell me that's changed after one small brush with stardom?'

Laura gave a sheepish smile. As everyone who knew her knew, she was obsessed with both fictional investigators like Detective Inspector Walker, and real detectives like her uncle. He'd been Scotland's top detective for five years running before he'd lost his wife while leading the hunt for the Straight As, one of the world's most notorious gangs. Devastated and blaming himself, he'd quit his job and fled to Cornwall. Now he worked as an undercover investigator for the Fisheries Inspectorate.

'Of course I'm not going to give up on my dream. It's just that acting did sound fun, that's all, and it would have been cool to see our names up in lights. Plus Tariq was practically turning cartwheels he was so excited about seeing Russia. Now I suppose you're not going to let us go.'

'On the contrary, I'd love you to go.'

Laura gave a squeal of delight. 'You're kidding?'

Calvin Redfern cut two slices of their housekeeper Rowenna's legendary apple pie, doused them in custard, and pushed a bowl over to Laura. 'No, I'm not. To tell you the truth, I have some news myself. I've been trying to pluck up the courage to break it to you.'

'What news?' The last six months had been the best of Laura's life. Living in glorious St Ives with the uncle she'd come to adore and her beloved husky was nothing short of magical. Meeting Tariq had been the icing on the cake. A little part of Laura was always slightly fearful that some twist of fate would return her to the Sylvan Meadows Home for Girls.

'Don't worry. It's not bad news, just bad timing. You may have heard that Britain's Deputy Prime Minister, Edward Lucas, is going on a rare state visit to Russia in the next couple of weeks. He'll be in Moscow, not St Petersburg, which is where you'll be filming if you do decide you're willing to be an extra. The two cities are a considerable distance apart, so it's unlikely that you'll even be aware he's in the country. That's probably not a bad thing. There's always tons of security surrounding these events.'

'I don't understand. What does Ed Lucas' visit have to do with you?'

Her uncle swallowed a mouthful of pie. 'As you know, I had a lot of experience working with criminal gangs like the Straight As when I was in the police force.'

Laura said nothing. Just the name of the gang was enough to make the hair stand up on the back of her neck. The Straight As were criminal masterminds with their fingers in hundreds of evil pies. Depending on your point of view, they were the best of the best or the worst of the worst. From bank robberies and horse race fixing to slave labour and black market dealing in endangered species, they were involved in all of it. On three occasions, she and Tariq had made the mistake of crossing them. Each time they'd almost paid with their lives.

'Go on.'

'A month ago, I was contacted by MI5. They've had reliable intelligence that the Russian mafia is planning an assassination attempt on Ed Lucas during his visit. For diplomatic reasons it's essential that the trip goes ahead so the Foreign Office has asked me, as an expert on criminal networks, to work with them to keep him safe.'

'How are you planning to track the potential assassin down?' Laura said excitedly, momentarily forgetting the Straight As. She loved intrigue. 'Do you have to go to Moscow?'

'No, I don't. But the powers that be do want me to base myself in London while Ed Lucas is in Russia so that I can head up the British side of the security operation. I did my best to refuse the assignment on the grounds that I've left that life behind, but they've gone to great lengths and offered me quite a bit of money in order to persuade me to agree.

'I'm sorry, Laura. I've been dreading telling you that I'd be away for several weeks in the middle of your school holidays. I know you think I'm a workaholic.'

'Yes, you are,' Laura scolded.

He smiled wryly. 'But don't you see that if you and Tariq are interested in working on the film, it could be the perfect solution for everyone? I've checked out the film studio, Tiger Pictures, and they have a good reputation in the business. They had some financial trouble but they're fine now. Brett Avery is a temperamental character, but he's generally well-liked and respected. He has also given me his word that Kay Allbright, your screenwriting friend, would be personally responsible for your welfare. We had a long conversation this morning and she seems a lovely person. Perhaps most importantly, you'd have Skye with you. And as Ana María Tyler discovered, there could be no better bodyguard.'

Beneath the kitchen table, the husky's tail thumped a happy rhythm. Laura rubbed his ears. Tariq's foster dad, a vet, had examined him thoroughly after his hundred and twenty-seven metre leap. Incredibly, he was no worse for wear. His heroics had made him the talk of the town, and the local paper had sent a photographer round to snap his picture.

'So there's only one question remaining,' Calvin Redfern was saying.

'Which is?'

'Would you like to go to Russia or not? Do you want to spend ten days working as a background artiste in one of the world's most fascinating cities – all expenses paid and with Skye and Tariq at your side – or would you prefer to spend your whole summer on the beach in beautiful St Ives?'

Laura glanced at the rain pouring down outside the window. If sunshine could be guaranteed, there'd be no contest. She'd choose to laze away the holidays on Porthmeor Beach. Annoyingly, it had been the wettest June since records began and now July was looking equally dismal.

On the other hand, St Petersburg, a city that conjured images of great monuments, magical nights at the ballet and long visits to the Hermitage Museum, a treasure house of art, sounded impossibly glamorous. So did working on a film set, even if she and Tariq did occupy the decidedly unglamorous roles of 'Girl in Red Hat' and 'Boy Pushing Cart.'

She smiled. 'I'd love to go to St Petersburg, but only if Tariq can come too.'

Her uncle poured more custard on her pie. 'Oh, I don't think you need have any worries on that score. Tariq's foster parents are both busy people and they think this would be a wonderful opportunity for him to see St Petersburg for free and have an unforgettable experience. Besides, they know the two of you are inseparable.'

There was a moment of silence as each contemplated that the reason Rob and Rena were so relaxed about Tariq's adventures with Laura was that they were blissfully unaware they'd frequently included encounters with kidnappers, bank robbers, volcanoes, sharks and other lethal things. For reasons of national security, those had been kept secret.

'So that's settled,' Laura said. For reasons unknown, butterflies started flapping around her stomach. She'd been uneasy since she'd left the film set the previous day, but she couldn't figure out why.

Her uncle carried the plates and mugs to the sink and began to wash up. 'Yes, that's settled, but on one condition.'

'I thought there might be a catch.'

'No catch but I want you to promise me you'll stay out of trouble. All foreign countries have the potential to be dangerous, but Russia is more deadly than most.'

Laura hopped up and pretended a sudden interest in drying dishes. How could she give him her word when trouble had a habit of seeking her out? Her day on the film set was a perfect example. One minute she was happily watching a young actress pick wild flowers, the next her husky was embroiled in a life and death drama.

'Laura?'

Her dimples deepened. 'Oh Uncle Calvin, there's not going to be any trouble. We'll be on a Hollywood film set, being taken care of twenty-four/seven. And as you said, Skye is the best bodyguard in the business.'

He laughed as he handed her a plate, his powerful forearms soapy with suds. 'I'm sure you're right. At least promise me that you'll make a holiday of it and enjoy yourself and not go looking for mysteries where there are none.'

Laura relaxed. Now that she could do. 'I promise.'

~ 4 ~

'WILL IT BE SNOWING, or should I take shorts?' asked Laura, gazing helplessly into her wardrobe. 'What about jeans? Will I need two pairs or three? And how on earth am I going to fit Skye's food dish and doggie treats into my suitcase? I've barely started packing and already it weighs a ton.'

Tariq was stretched out on her duvet, using the husky's furry hindquarters as a pillow. He glanced up from the pages of his Russian guidebook.

'According to this, St Petersburg is the world's northernmost city and we're going to be there during the famous White Nights. Apparently it's light almost twenty-four hours a day and the sun barely dips below the horizon. How cool is that? Some people don't bother going to bed at all. They stroll along the Neva River or hang out in cafes or at the Hermitage, which is one of the largest art museums in the world. It has over three million works of art.'

'Sounds great, but now I'm even more confused. Are they called the White Nights because they're freezing, or is it like summer all evening long? Or something in between?'

'The guidebook says the temperature could be anywhere from thirteen degrees to twenty-three. I've taken every bit of clothing I own, which isn't very much, and you should do the same. I don't think it'll be hot enough for shorts and you probably won't need treats. They do have dogs in Russia, you know. There are bound to be pet shops selling food.'

'Yes, but these are his favourites and— '

The doorbell drowned the rest of the sentence. Lottie's booming bark echoed up the stairs.

Skye bounded off the bed and out of the room. Tariq sat up. 'Are you expecting someone?'

Laura shut the suitcase. 'Not as far as I know. My uncle would have mentioned it before he left for work this morning. Maybe it's the postman.'

She hurried down, followed by Tariq. Skye and Lottie were growling and snuffling at the front door. Laura peered through the spyhole. A bouquet of flowers blocked the way, obscuring the person holding them.

Laura backed away from the door. The last time someone

had come to number 28 with a delivery, it was a ruse by the Straight A gang to kidnap her. It was not an experience she was anxious to repeat.

'What is it?' Tariq peered through the spyhole as the doorbell rang again and Lottie let off another volley of deafening barks. 'That's weird.'

'What's weird?'

'It's the stunt coordinator from the film set. What do you suppose he wants?'

'I don't know, but whatever it is it must be urgent.'

Laura unlocked the door and opened it with a smile. The man was already halfway down the steps. When she called out to him he turned with a strange reluctance, almost as if he'd changed his mind and would have preferred there to be no one home.

'Excuse me! Sorry it took me so long to answer the door. Can I help you?'

'I, um, these are for you, Miss Marlin.' He thrust the flowers at her. 'To say thanks. I don't know if you remember me from the set. I'm Andre March, the stunt coordinator.'

Laura was astonished. She stared up at him through a fragrant thicket of poppies, roses and cornflowers. 'It's very kind of you, but I can't think of anything I've done to deserve them.'

He looked from her to Tariq, who stood protectively at the top of the steps gripping Skye's collar. 'It's not so much what you've done, it's what your husky did. He saved Ana María's life. If it hadn't been for him, I'd never have worked again in this industry. My life would have been ruined. As it is, I'm quitting. Brett Avery hasn't fired me, but it's been made clear to me that I should go.'

Laura's heart went out to him. 'I'm so sorry. I feel responsible. You see, Skye, my husky, he sort of caused the accident by chasing the Pomeranian. He thought she was a toy. It's my fault. I should have been holding him tighter.'

A storm was closing in and a sharp, cool breeze preceded it, yet beads of sweat had broken out on Andre's forehead. He wiped them away with the sleeve of his shirt. Glancing with agitation at Laura's neighbour, Mrs Crabtree, who'd chosen that exact moment to dash into her garden and rescue her laundry from the line, he said in a low voice: 'Is it possible to go inside so we can talk more privately?'

It was on the tip of Laura's tongue to refuse. Stranger danger and all that. But then he added: 'Your friend and dogs are welcome to hear what I have to say. I mean you no harm. I only want to return the favour you have done me.'

'Gorgeous flowers, Laura!' cried Mrs Crabtree, Laura's neighbour, who was dressed entirely in purple. 'Are those from the film studio? Don't tell me you're getting the star treatment already? Does that extend to "background artistes"? In my day, there was no such thing. People who appeared in crowd scenes were known as extras and appeared in the credits with titles like "Girl Sweeping Street" or "Limping Pickpocket". They didn't get flowers and free holidays to St Petersburg. But perhaps that's your reward for Skye's heroics. That Ana María what-you-may-call-it could have plunged to her death . . .'

Pellets of rain splattered down on Laura's arm.

'Excuse us, Mrs Crabtree,' she said, virtually shoving Andre up the steps. 'We have an urgent appointment with the film's stunt coordinator.'

'Stunts? I do hope you're insured . . .'

Mercifully, the rain came slanting in, forcing Mrs Crabtree to pick up her washing and flee. Laura and Andre bolted inside, followed by Tariq and Skye. Lottie growled and barked until Laura quieted her. Ordinarily she would never have dreamt of inviting a near stranger into the house without her uncle present, but she had plenty of protection, plus her neighbour as a witness.

'Can I offer you a drink? We have tea or coffee or juice. I think it's mango.'

Andre shook his head vigorously and held his position near the door. 'I can't stay. I wanted only . . .' He stopped. 'This is a mistake. I should go.'

'It's okay,' Tariq reassured him. 'The dogs won't bite and nor will we.'

'Are you sure I can't get you a glass of water?' asked Laura. 'You don't look well at all. Do you have a migraine or something? Please don't worry about returning any favours. I'm glad that Skye saved the day, but he acted on instinct. It had nothing to do with me.'

'Maybe, but he's your dog. I owe you both. The only thing is . . .' His sleeve flew up and mopped more beads of sweat. 'Well, I'm not sure you'll thank me for it. You'll think I'm mad, just like the rest of the crew.'

Laura exchanged glances with Tariq. She regretted allowing Andre to enter the house. He was acting so oddly that she couldn't blame his colleagues for believing he was slightly deranged. 'Of course we won't think you're mad,' she lied. 'What did you want to tell us?'

'Go on,' Tariq encouraged.

Andre took a deep breath. 'Do you know that there are films which are said to be cursed?'

'I've never heard of a movie being cursed, but I've just done a school project on Egyptology and that involved a curse,' said Tariq. 'When the archaeologist, Howard Carter, opened Tutankhamun's tomb in 1923, loads of spooky things happened. Almost everyone who was at the opening of the tomb later fell victim to accidents, unexplained illnesses and even deaths.'

Andre was impressed. 'I actually worked on a documentary about Tutankhamun so I'm familiar with the stories about an ancient curse sent to destroy anyone who disturbed the boy king's tomb. Our research proved that almost all of them were conspiracy theories. I mean, Carter himself died of old age. The only really creepy story is the one about Lord Carnarvon, the man who financed the dig. He was bitten by a mosquito during the opening of the tomb. The bite became infected and he fell seriously ill. At the exact moment that he passed away in Egypt, his dog in England gave a series of blood-curdling howls and dropped down dead.'

Skye, who'd been regarding Andre with his vivid blue eyes, cocked his head and whined, sending a shiver up Laura's spine. The stunt manager nearly jumped out of his skin.

'Yes, but what does that have to do with your film?'

demanded Laura, determined to keep the conversation in touch with reality. 'Are you saying that *The Aristocratic Thief* is cursed?'

'Not the film, the set. For years, I've heard stories about film sets that seem to attract one disaster after another. Most relate to horror films like *The Crow*. Not being a fan of them myself, I've always taken these tales with a pinch of salt. Some are more believable than others, but I've always believed that even those that are proven to be genuine are linked only by coincidence.

'When the film *The Crow* was being made, there were lots of bizarre happenings, including a fire and an electrocution and Brandon Lee, the son of martial arts legend Bruce Lee, was tragically killed by a gun that was supposed to be loaded only with blank cartridges.

'When the James Bond movie, *Quantum of Solace*, was being filmed, Daniel Craig, who plays Bond, cut his face and needed eight stitches. A week later he sliced off the top of his finger doing a stunt. There was also a fire on the set and two stuntmen were hurt in separate car accidents. One mysteriously drove an Aston Martin sports car into Lake Garda in Italy.'

Sensing Laura's impatience, he said quickly: 'I am getting to the point. You may have noticed that when Ana María was in trouble on the cliff yesterday, I seemed confused. Normally, I can assure you I am the opposite. My job depends on my staying calm in a crisis. Every day I supervise stuntmen and actors as they set themselves on fire, endure car crashes and throw themselves off cliffs.'

Tariq was puzzled. 'But none of those things are real, are they? They're all staged for effect.'

'Yes, they are. But many stunts can be life-threatening if they're not done correctly.'

'What went wrong yesterday?' asked Laura.

A small smile lightened the gloom on Andre's face. 'You mean, apart from your husky deciding that Britney would make a delicious snack?'

'Yes, apart from that.'

'Three things – all potentially lethal.' He counted them off on his fingers. 'One, the ropes on my harness were cut.'

The blood quickened in Laura's veins. Finally, they were getting somewhere. 'Deliberately? I mean, they weren't worn out or anything?'

He gave her a cutting look, as if to say, Give me credit. I'm a professional.

'They had been sliced with a knife *on purpose*. You don't get much more deliberate than that. Two, when I abseiled down the cliff later that day to try to work out why the stunt had been such a disaster, I found that the ledge Ana María was standing on – a ledge I'd built myself – had been unscrewed in two places. That meant it was unable to support her weight. Three, the centre of the safety net had been carefully frayed with a razor. Even if she'd landed in it, she'd have fallen straight through.'

Tariq was aghast. 'Someone was trying to kill her?'

'If those were the only things that had gone wrong since we started filming, I'd have jumped to the same conclusion. But they're not. There have been so many strange incidents that I hardly know where to start. On the night before we left Los Angeles, five of our crew members came down with food-poisoning so severe we had to leave them behind.

'And it didn't end there; on our first evening in St Ives, our cinematographer tripped over a chair that had been overturned in a dark passage and broke both his wrists. Then yesterday an unidentified car travelling at high speed veered in front of our equipment truck, causing it to overturn. Incredibly, the truck driver suffered only minor injuries. However, thousands of pounds worth of equipment was destroyed.'

'Do you have any idea who or what is behind this?' Laura asked. 'You talk about the set being cursed. Do you think it's haunted?'

He gave a hollow laugh. 'Miss Marlin, I do not believe in ghosts, evil spirits or anything else supernatural or fantastical. I *do* believe that someone – a human being – wants the film stopped, and will go to any lengths to make that happen.'

'But who would take such desperate measures?' asked Tariq.

'And why?' added Laura.

'I don't know and I don't plan to hang around and find out.' Andre glanced anxiously at his watch. 'I'm leaving on the 2.33 p.m. train to Newquay. I can't miss it. The sooner I'm back in LA, the better I'll like it. But I couldn't go without warning you. You and your husky must quit the film at once. If you go to Russia,

I believe that something terrible will happen.'

Laura almost laughed. 'We can't. We've signed a contract.'

'And the film company have given us our plane tickets and booked our hotel rooms,' added Tariq. 'There's a car taking us to the airport tomorrow. It's all arranged.'

'Then unarrange it. Your lives may depend on it. You're only extras. It's not as if you'll be missed.'

'Gee, thanks,' Laura said drily, 'but aren't you forgetting something?'

She put a hand on Skye's head. He was watching their faces as if he understood every word. 'We might not be missed, but Skye will. Brett Avery has paid a fortune in visa fees and transport arrangements for him. I doubt if one penny of it is refundable. Even if we wanted to get out of the contract, which we don't, he'd probably sue my uncle. There's no way I'm going to let that happen just because of a few weird incidents that may not even be connected.'

'Nor me,' Tariq said firmly.

Laura smiled. 'Thanks for coming here today, Andre. We'll go to St Petersburg, but don't worry, we'll be careful. What's that saying? "Forewarned is forearmed". We'll watch our backs.'

Andre's mouth set in an angry line. 'Well, so be it. Let no one accuse me of not doing my duty. I'll go with a clear conscience, but I believe you're making a serious mistake. There are many ways you could get out of your contract. You could feign illness or even wrap your husky's paw in a bandage and claim it's broken. If you do nothing and something bad happens, you only have yourselves to blame.'

He pulled open the front door with an expression that was close to dread. 'Good luck, Miss Marlin. You'll need it.'

~ 5 ~

LAURA PRESSED HER nose to window of the British Airways jet and gazed out at the Russian landscape rising to meet them. It was flat, parched and dotted with factories. A bronze lake sparkled in the distance. As the plane touched down on the runway, spiky fir trees, like upended brooms, sped by.

'Do you think we've done the right thing – ignoring Andre's warning and coming here?' Tariq asked as they waited for their luggage. Their passports had been stamped by an unsmiling official with stars on the epaulettes of his white uniform.

'Firstly, we didn't exactly have a choice,' Laura said. 'We

had signed a contract and the tickets were bought and everything was arranged. Secondly, we have a mystery to solve. It'll give us something to do during the long hours when we're not needed for filming. Sounds as if there'll be quite a few of those.'

'I thought your uncle told you to stay out of trouble.'

'He did, but he also instructed us – several times – to look after each other and keep each other safe. If I didn't at least do a little bit of investigating to make absolutely sure that somebody isn't about to drop a brick on your head or poison Skye, I'd be breaking my promise to him.'

'What's all this talk about poisoning and dropping bricks?' demanded Kay, coming over to them with a trolley. 'You've been reading too many detective novels. I visited St Petersburg when I was researching *The Aristocratic Thief* and found it one of the most civilised cities on earth and among the most beautiful. Quite glorious. Wait until you see it.'

For most of the long drive from the airport, Laura thought that both Kay and the author of the guidebook needed glasses if they considered the place attractive. Initially, everything seemed a universal grey. Soulless concrete buildings crowded wide motorways, over which flyovers looped like fighting snakes. A giant statue of Vladimir Lenin, the communist revolutionary who rose to become ruler of the Soviet Union in the 1920s, towered over the traffic. A thick coating of brown dust made the cars and buildings look duller still.

Laura cuddled Skye, who'd jumped into the back seat between her and Tariq after they'd collected him from the cargo division and bared his teeth when the film company driver, a surly Russian who spoke little English, objected.

Laura had apologised but refused to move her husky, explaining that he needed to be close to her after the long, scary flight. 'He's very gentle really. It's just that he's been travelling for about twenty-four hours and he's out of sorts.'

Kay supported her by telling the driver that Skye was no ordinary husky. 'Back in England, he saved a young girl's life. What's more, he is about to become as famous as Lassie. Have you heard of Lassie? No? Look, if it makes you feel better, he can sit on my coat, but we are absolutely not leaving the airport without him. He's one of us and he's going to ride with us.'

As the driver started the engine with a snarl that rivalled Skye's, Laura warmed to Kay even more. There was something so straightforward, decent and warm about the screenwriter that it was impossible not to like her.

It wasn't until they swept through the city gates that a sense of wonder came over Laura. It was as if they'd stepped through a magic curtain into another world. Within moments they were cruising along tree-lined boulevards overlooked on all sides by magnificent architecture. It was as if the best buildings and monuments from Paris, Rome, Prague, London and other great cities had been scooped up by the founder of the city, Tsar Peter the Great, and deposited in St Petersburg.

The colours changed too. A mansion of dusky pink, edged with cream, flanked a pale green restaurant. In among the statues, there were museums, homes and shops painted rusty red or baby blue or mustard yellow. As they drove into the city centre, further delights awaited them. Horse-drawn carriages clip-clopped past canals alive with riverboats, swans and wild ducks. It was nearly 7 p.m. and yet the sun was still shining and the sky an electric blue.

'Would you believe that the city's name has been changed three times?' said Kay. 'In 1914 it was renamed Petrograd, then a decade later it was altered to Leningrad. It wasn't until the 1990s that it was called St Petersburg again. Personally, that's my favourite.'

The drive took nearly an hour and Laura was glad to reach the Pushka Inn, which would be their home for the next ten days. She was even happier when she saw the room she'd be sharing with Kay and Skye. A chandelier twinkled on the ceiling, and red velvet drapes framed the French doors. She chose the bed by the window, which was so soft it almost swallowed her when she sat on it. The bathroom was pink and white and had a Jacuzzi-style tub.

Best of all was the balcony, which overhung a canal. Skye rushed out and growled hungrily at a swan gliding by.

'I'll feed you in a minute and take you for a nice walk,' Laura told him, 'but only if you promise to stay away from all small creatures. And large ones. They have bears in Russia. I don't want you being eaten.'

Tariq, who was in an adjoining single room on his own, came out to join her. 'My bed is so big I'm worried I might get lost in it. Would it be all right if I borrowed Skye for the night?'

'Sure. As long as you understand that it's like sleeping with a furry hot water bottle. Given half a chance, he'll try to share your pillow.'

'Isn't this wonderful?' cried Kay, stepping out into the sunshine. 'We're on the roof of the world. That's where St Petersburg is on the map, you know, level with Helsinki in Finland. We're so close to the Arctic, we could almost reach out and touch it.'

She hooked her arm through Laura's. 'Come along, roomie. Let's feed your beautiful wolf and then I'll treat you and Tariq to dinner.'

It was after ten when Laura finally brushed her teeth and put on her pyjamas. She was physically weary but somehow wide awake, which might have had something to do with the hot chocolate she'd had with her meal. It was so thick she'd had to eat it with a spoon. On the basis of that alone, Laura had already decided that, next to St Ives, St Petersburg was her favourite place in the world.

'It's awesome,' she'd told her uncle when he'd called as they were walking back to the hotel. 'The hotel is beautiful and the food is delicious. I thought we'd be eating boiled cabbage and potato soup every night, but we had beetroot soup. Borscht, it's called. You eat it with sour cream and black rye bread. It sounds revolting, but it's totally divine. Then we had apple pie and this hot chocolate to die for.'

He laughed. 'I'm happy to hear it. St Petersburg has

always been high on my list of cities to visit. Well, spare a thought for your poor uncle. I'm staying in a London hotel that has all the charm of a maximum security prison and working round the clock to organise the security for Ed Lucas' visit. It's a nightmare. He's a nightmare. You'd think he actually wanted to be assassinated. He's behaving as if he's going on holiday. Wants to visit this museum and that gallery, and eat at such and such a restaurant. He leaves for Moscow early tomorrow morning and the arrangements are not even fifty per cent completed.'

'He sounds like a pain in the neck. But if anyone can protect him, it's you.'

'I hope you're right. Sleep well, Laura, and say hi to Skye and Tariq. I miss you all.'

'We miss you too, Uncle Calvin. I wish you could be with us.'

'So do I, Laura. So do I.'

Laura rinsed the toothpaste out of her mouth and studied herself in the bathroom mirror. Her uncle often remarked that with her cap of short blonde hair and serious grey eyes, she was the image of her mother, his sister, who'd died when Laura was born. Of her father, reputed to be an American sailor, there'd never been any sign. For years Laura had dreamed that he'd materialise one day at the Sylvan Meadows Home for Girls and take her away to a loving family home. Now she was glad he hadn't. Calvin Redfern was the best dad any mystery-mad girl who had ambitions of becoming a detective could ever have hoped for.

For that reason, she felt guilty that she'd said nothing to

him about Andre's visit, let alone his warning. She'd justified this omission by telling herself that her uncle had other, more important, things on his mind. But the real reason she hadn't mentioned it was that she was scared he might ban her and Tariq from getting on the plane to Russia.

There was a rap on the bathroom door. 'Are you okay in there, Laura, or have you disappeared down the plughole?'

Laura emerged with a grin. 'Sorry, Kay. The bathroom is the place where I do my best thinking.'

'In that case, I'll be using the bathroom first in future. Then you'll be able to do your thinking at your own leisure.'

Laura laughed and hopped into the wonderfully soft bed. Skye was in the room next door with Tariq. It felt strange to be thinking of sleep when the sun was still beaming outside. She picked up the guidebook and began to read about the famous St Petersburg White Nights. She must have dozed off almost immediately, because she was awoken a few minutes later by Kay's voice.

'Did you put this here, Laura, or do you think it's a peculiar local custom to welcome guests with a card?'

Laura's eyes snapped open. Kay was sitting on the edge of her bed, holding a playing card. It wasn't just any playing card. It was a meticulously painted Joker wearing a malevolent grin.

Her blood ran cold. 'Where did you find it?'

'Here – tucked between the pillow and the duvet. Why? What on earth's wrong? You look quite ill.'

Before going out to the restaurant, Laura had left her pyjamas lying on Kay's bed. Anyone entering the room – a spying member of the housekeeping staff, for instance –

would have automatically assumed that she'd be the one sleeping on that side of the room, not Kay. Laura's face felt as frozen as a death mask, but she forced a smile. 'I think the long day has caught up with me. I'm shattered. Uh, would you mind if I looked at the card?'

Kay yawned. 'Be my guest, but it's lights-out time in about thirty seconds. If I stay up any longer, I'll turn into a pumpkin.'

Laura took the card from her, feeling a shiver go through her at the mere touch of it. It was like holding a small slice of evil. Kay couldn't know – and Laura was not about to enlighten her – that the Joker was the calling card of the Straight As. Nor could she know that the gang had sworn vengeance against Laura, Tariq and Calvin Redfern for their role in the capture of various high-ranking members.

Throughout these arrests, the mastermind behind the Straight As, a mysterious figure known only as Mr A, had remained elusive. For those seeking justice, it didn't help that no law enforcement officer anywhere in the world had any idea what he looked like. Even his own gang members claimed never to have seen him. He controlled every division of the Straight As from afar, via the Internet and coded messages – a spider at the centre of a sinister web.

Rather chillingly, Mr A did, it seemed, recognise Laura. He'd even texted her in June after she'd helped foil a bank robbery in Kentucky. It was those words that returned to haunt Laura now.

Bravo Laura Marlin! You are a worthy adversary. Until we meet again . . . Mr A

'Night night,' Kay said sleepily, switching off the light. 'Sweet dreams.'

But dreams of any kind were impossible for Laura. She lay stiff and cold in the darkness, wishing Skye was with her and not sleeping beside Tariq in the next room.

The card was a message meant for her, of that she did not have a sliver of doubt. The Straight As knew she was in Russia. They were waiting for her.

~ 6 ~

'**WE SHOULD NEVER** have come,' Laura told Tariq over breakfast when Kay left the table to visit the buffet counter. 'We should have taken Andre's advice and made up some excuse about Skye being ill or injured. There are thousands of Siberian huskies in Russia. One of them must have a missing front leg.'

She paused as the waitress arrived with two plates piled high with golden crêpes. Tariq's smile could have lit up the room. He immediately spooned honey and sour cream over his portion. Laura regretted ordering hers. She felt ill with tiredness and worry.

'We could have made up a story to get out of our

contract,' conceded Tariq, 'but it would have been dishonest. Besides, we were excited about coming. You said it would be an adventure.'

'That was before I knew that the Straight As were lying in wait for us. Now I want to catch the next flight home.'

Tariq's fork paused on the way to his mouth. 'Laura Marlin, I can't believe you just said that. Is that what Matt Walker would do in this situation – run away?'

Laura studied a speck on the tablecloth. 'It wouldn't be running away, it would be . . . sensible.'

Tariq put a palm on her forehead. 'Your skin feels hot. I think you might be coming down with something. Either that, or a Russian alien has abducted my best friend.'

Laura pushed his hand away. 'Tariq, be serious. Think about what the Straight A gang have put us through. Because of them, we've been kidnapped twice, nearly drowned and almost been fried to a crisp by a volcano.'

He picked up his knife and fork and started work on the crêpes again. 'Yes, and we've survived all those things because of you. You're an amazing detective – at least as good as Matt Walker. Okay, let's say the card was a message for you. Calvin Redfern says that the Straight As leave the Joker as a kind of joke. It's their way of telling the police or anyone else trying to catch them that they've got a big job planned and they're confident they're going to get away with it.'

'And your point is?' Laura dipped a square of crêpe into the bowls of honey and sour cream and cautiously put it in her mouth. The combined flavours were unexpectedly wonderful.

'What would Matt Walker do in this situation?'

Laura ate a few more bites of crêpe as she considered. Her detective hero often took jobs that would allow him to keep an eye on a suspect until they made a move. Then he'd pounce. 'I guess he'd do what we're doing. He'd get a job that would allow him to blend in with the crowd and observe without being observed. He'd work undercover as a film extra, say.'

'Background artiste,' put in Tariq.

'Sorry, I keep forgetting. Yes, he'd work as a background artiste. And while he was doing that he'd also look into the string of accidents on set and find out whether or not there was anyone or anything behind them. I suppose the good thing about us having obscure parts in the movie is that we'll have plenty of time to slip off and explore St Petersburg and try to find out what the Straight As are up to. Unfortunately, the Joker card means that the Straight As are already watching us. That takes away any element of surprise. Unless . . .'

'Unless we pretend you never received it?'

'Exactly. If we act all happy and excited and continue as if absolutely nothing has happened, chances are they might let down their guard. In the past, they've only ever tried to harm us when we've got close to one of their operations. We could pretend that we're so caught up in the Hollywood dream and the wonders of St Petersburg that we no longer have any interest in solving mysteries.'

Tariq said teasingly, 'Does that mean that you're not going to be getting on the next plane back to England after all?'

'What – me? Of course not. Well, okay, it did cross my mind briefly, but then I remembered that Matt Walker has never walked away from anything in his life. Nor has my uncle. But, Tariq, we do need to be careful. If we see anything suspicious, we are absolutely not going to get involved. We are going to call Uncle Calvin immediately so he can alert the authorities.'

He saluted. 'Aye, aye, captain.'

'What are the two of you grinning about?' asked Kay, sitting down with a tray loaded with healthy options like plain yoghurt, fruit and muesli. 'You have a mischievous air about you. What are you planning?'

Laura gave her an angelic smile. 'Mischievous, us? Never. We're just preparing for our new roles. We might only be background artistes but we're going to be the best background artistes we can possibly be.'

To Laura, there was something surreal about emerging from the hotel to find that the ordinary street of the previous evening had been transformed into a historical scene by the film crew. There were stagecoaches and men striding about in smart waistcoats and breeches. A woman in a long red gown and fancy hat was talking on her mobile phone while drinking a coffee outside the catering trailer.

Nearby, an actor in a top hat played computer games on his iPad.

'To me, one of the peculiar delights of working on a period drama like *The Aristocratic Thief* is scenes like this,' said Kay. 'I find it funny when actors in nineteenth-century costumes do twenty-first century things like sit around eating hamburgers and drinking Coke, or playing *Angry Birds* on their mobiles.'

'What are you filming today?' asked Tariq.

'It's the scene where Oscar de Havier, the aristocratic thief of the story, meets the orphan girl, Violet, and her three-legged husky, Flash. As you already know, the girl is being played by Ana María and Flash will be played by Skye. In the scene, Violet almost goes under the wheels of Oscar's carriage. A confrontation ensues.'

She lowered her voice. 'That's William Raven, the actor who's been cast as Oscar de Havier – a controversial choice.'

Laura followed her gaze. A silver-haired man in a long black coat and boots polished to a high shine was talking to the director. Brett Avery had a notebook in his hand and was scribbling frantically. In theory, it was Brett who was the boss, not the other way round, but the actor's height and his handsome, arrogant face gave him a presence that made Brett's wiry frame seem shrunken and rather nerdy.

The director looked up and spotted them. Or rather, he spotted the husky. 'Kids! Kids! Bring Skye over here.'

'Any actor featuring in the next scene would usually be in hair and make-up by now, but Skye is gorgeous enough as he is,' Kay said with a laugh. 'Go and meet William Raven. I'd be interested to hear what you think.'

Not a lot, was Laura's opinion as they approached. The man's chilly gaze crawled over her and Tariq with the probing intensity of a prison searchlight.

'This is the dog I was telling you about,' Brett Avery was saying with boyish enthusiasm. 'And these are the lovely kids who own him. Fine young actors. Kids, meet the star of our film, William Raven – a future Hollywood legend if I have anything to do with it.'

Since he'd never seen them act, Laura suspected the director was exaggerating their importance to disguise the fact that he had obviously forgotten their names.

Brett patted Skye rather gingerly on the head. 'What do you think, William? He's quite a find, even if I say so myself. Audiences will be coming in droves to see him. Saved Ana María's life, you know. Jumped off a cliff and dragged her from the boiling sea. Extraordinary thing.'

The actor gave a practiced smile. 'So I heard. I hadn't realised he was disabled.'

Laura's temper flared. 'He's not disabled,' she snapped, 'and so what if he was. A car hit him when he was a puppy and they couldn't save his leg, but he's fifty times fitter, stronger and faster than most dogs with four legs, and a lot more useful than any human being I've ever come across – famous or not.'

Brett Avery became quite agitated. 'Of course he is, of course he is. Isn't that what I was saying? Umm, I hadn't realised how late it was. Would you excuse us, William?

I'm sure Laura didn't mean any offence. Apologies, sorry, umm, see you shortly.'

He steered the children away, gripping Laura's shoulder until she winced in protest. As soon as they were out of sight of the actor, he stopped and glared at them. Shoving his milk-bottle glasses up over the beak of his nose, he looked more like a cross crow than ever.

'You're new on the set, so I'm going to let you off with a warning. If you dare to speak to my star actor that way ever again, I'll have you escorted off the set by security and put on the first plane back to England. Do I make myself clear?'

'But he insulted Skye,' Laura said indignantly. 'I didn't offend him. He offended us.'

'I don't care if he says that your Great-Aunt Bertha resembles a whale. You grin and bear it. William Raven pays our salaries. At least, his movie producer brother does. Mr Raven is a man of – how shall I put it? – great sensitivity. As it is I'm going to have to do some fast-talking to prevent you being fired. If you upset him again and he walks out, the movie is finished and one hundred and fifty-six actors, extras and crew are out of work. Do I make myself understood?'

'Yes,' they mumbled in unison.

'Sorry,' added Laura.

'All right, let's put it behind us. If Mr Raven says jump, the only question you should be asking is: "How high?"' He checked his watch. 'Take Skye to Otto, the animal trainer, as quickly as you can. He's needed in the next scene.'

'What about us?' asked Tariq. 'Are we needed?'

'Most definitely not. You're lucky I haven't thrown you off my set. Stay away from my crew and my actors and don't speak unless you're spoken to.'

'YOU WERE BARELY out of my sight for five minutes – how on earth did you manage to upset the great William Raven?'

Laura's heart sank. The last thing she wanted to do was fall out with Kay, their only friend in Russia. She was about to launch into a stumbling apology when the scriptwriter poked her in the ribs and giggled.

'Don't fret. I don't blame you in the least. What a nerve the man has. Skye is worth a hundred of him. Anyway, I'm glad someone finally stood up to him. Ever since filming began, he's been treating everyone, including Brett, as if they were the hired help. Look at the way he's being helped into the carriage for the next scene. Anyone would think he was a real aristocrat, not an actor merely playing one.'

Putting her arms around their shoulders, she led them over to a silver equipment case, where they could perch and watch the production team set up a street market scene. The carriage was parked some distance away. Tariq, who adored horses, was transfixed by the magnificent black pair being hitched to it. It was a warm blue day and their necks were already streaked with sweat. A worried groom wiped them down and combed their manes.

Across the street, Skye was sitting obediently beside Otto, the animal handler. For Laura, it was an odd feeling watching someone else handle Skye, but it helped knowing that Otto genuinely loved animals. The husky seemed quite content. From time to time, he glanced at Laura, but for the most part he, like Tariq, was riveted by the frenetic activity on the street.

As they waited, Chad MacFarlane, a teenager from California, grudgingly delivered a cold drink to William Raven. Chad had the head-turning good looks of a high school football star or a boy band member, but his whole demeanour seemed to say that he considered his job as a runner – a film set dogsbody – beneath him. Laura got the feeling that he was only doing it in the hope of being snapped up by a talent scout and turned into a superstar. According to Kay, his coffee was undrinkable and his sandwich-making skills non-existent.

William Raven settled back in his carriage seat and put on the hat and cape that transformed him into the aristocrat, Oscar de Havier.

Laura said casually, 'Kay, you told us earlier that

Mr Raven was a controversial choice for the role. Why is that?'

Kay glanced over her shoulder. 'If I tell you, it's confidential and can go no further than the three of us. Deal?'

'Deal.'

'You have our word,' Tariq assured her.

'It all started six weeks ago, the day before we were due to fly to the UK to begin filming. The movie was cast, the crew was hired, and we were packed and ready to go. Next morning we arrived at the film studio to find several staff members in tears. Tiger Pictures had gone bust, seemingly over night. As if that wasn't bad enough, our lead actor, a huge Hollywood star – I could tell you his name but I'd have to kill you afterwards – had pulled out with no explanation.

'We were all devastated, particularly Brett and I. We'd spent about five years fighting to get the movie to happen. The *Hollywood Reporter* ran a story on our woes. Within days, something miraculous happened. We were approached by a new production company. Not only were they prepared to finance the film, they were prepared to release the money overnight. To begin with, we kept looking for a catch, but there was none. Mick Edwards, the new producer, had only one condition.'

'He wanted you to cast a family member or friend as the star of the film,' Tariq guessed.

'Smart boy. That's exactly right. William Raven is a fine actor, so it wasn't his talent we doubted, but for marketing reasons we'd rather have had an established Hollywood star. We also knew that the reason Mr Raven hasn't become a household name is that audiences tend to react badly to him. They find him cold.'

Laura watched the actor climbing into the carriage in preparation for the next scene. He was too far away for her to see his expression, but she could still recall how her skin had crawled under his piercing stare. 'Yes, I can imagine.'

'Unfortunately, we didn't have a choice. We were basically ordered to hire him. At the time he was working as a conjurer and that didn't exactly fill us with confidence, but we were between a rock and a hard place. Either Brett and I walked away from everything we'd spent five long years working towards or we agreed to have William be our star. For better or worse, we said yes.'

'Which has it been so far?' asked Tariq. 'Better or worse?'

'To be truthful, apart from being a bit of a prima donna, William has been great. He's the least of our worries. There've been a string of other incidents that have caused us much more of a headache. Nothing you need to concern yourself with. They're trifling things really. Oh, look, they're about to start shooting.'

Before Laura could press her on the headache-causing incidents, which she guessed were the ones that had so unnerved Andre March, someone yelled 'Action!' The cameras rolled.

Ana María, dressed once more as the orphan Violet, led Skye along a pavement packed with raggedy market traders. There were stalls laden with fruit and vegetables, and others selling cheese, sausages, oil lamps, and reams of colourful cloth. A boy with a grubby face begged for bread.

Along the cobbled street came the shining carriage, pulled by the proud black horses. Their necks arched and their manes flew as they trotted past the market stalls, urged on by the driver's swinging whip. Oscar de Havier was visible only as a shadow in the rear of the carriage.

As the carriage rattled up the street, a man carrying a load of chickens swung his crate and knocked Ana María into the path of the horses.

That part was scripted. Unfortunately the crate door flew open and one of the chickens flapped out. It tore squawking into the street. The horses shied violently, unseating the driver, who crashed to the ground. William Raven's terrified face appeared briefly at the window before the carriage careered away down the street, dragged by the out-of-control horses.

Everyone started shrieking and panicking at once.

Kay sprang off the equipment case. 'Oh my goodness. This can't be happening. Laura, quick! Run and grab Skye before he adds to the chaos by chasing the chicken.'

'Do something, Otto,' screamed Brett Avery. 'Stop the horses! Save William! If the carriage reaches the main road, they'll all be killed.'

Unfortunately, Otto was a beachball of a man who became short of breath if he saw someone running on the television. He was not physically equipped to be a hero. All he did was bleat despairingly and clutch at his few remaining tufts of hair. Further along the road, a couple of brawny crew members tried to grab the reins as the horses galloped by. The beasts swerved, causing the carriage to rock wildly.

Their groom pursued them, but he was a tall, ungainly man, not built for running, and the horses effortlessly outdistanced him.

William's desperate cries grew fainter. 'Somebody save me! HE-ELP!'

'I'll do it,' Tariq said suddenly.

Before Kay could stop him, he was sprinting across the production unit car park, dodging trucks and hurdling fat coils of black cable. He was taking a shortcut in a bid to reach the horses before they got to the main road.

With the exception of Kay and Laura, nobody noticed him. Most people were too busy watching the carriage being dragged full-pelt toward certain disaster.

Brett Avery was apoplectic. 'Do something, you idiots!' he yelled at no one in particular. 'Oh, I'm ruined. Totally ruined.'

Laura held tightly to Skye's collar and squinted into the sunlight, her heart in her mouth. It didn't seem possible that Tariq could reach the crazed horses before the traffic engulfed them. Even if he did, she dreaded to think what would happen to him. The few people brave enough to attempt to halt the horses had either been tossed aside or trampled. One had a bad cut on his leg and the other looked as if he'd been attacked by wild boars. The coach driver was unconscious.

Kay was beside herself. 'What does Tariq think he's doing? If he winds up in the emergency room, it'll be my responsibility.'

Overhearing her, one of the cameramen swung his lens in the direction of the running figure. The red recording light glowed. 'Now that's impressive. I don't think I've ever seen a kid run so fast. He's like an Olympic sprinter. I wouldn't worry about his health though. He has no chance of cutting off the horses. By the time he's crossed the bridge, they'll be . . . I don't believe it. I don't believe the evidence of my own eyes.'

Neither did Laura. Realising that he had no chance of cutting off the runaways if he used the canal bridge fifty metres away, Tariq had leapt off the riverbank onto a moving barge. Ignoring the outraged shouts of the tour guide, who was in the midst of explaining the wonders of St Petersburg to twenty-eight Japanese tourists, he ran the length of the vessel and jumped onto a moored speedboat.

From there, he sprang onto a rowing boat. It was bucking on the waves generated by the barge and Tariq almost went headfirst into the water, but managed to save himself by grabbing an iron rung in the canal wall. By the time he'd hauled himself onto the bank, word had spread across the film set. The cameras were rolling and everyone was transfixed.

'He's going to get hisself killed, no question about it,' said a woman dressed as a market trader.

Tariq stood directly in the path of the horses, close to the thundering traffic. Kay had her hands over her eyes and was peering through her fingers. 'Please tell me he's not going to offer himself up as a sort of human shield. He'll be crushed to death.'

'You don't know Tariq,' Laura said loyally. 'He has a gift

with horses – with all animals. They won't hurt him. They can't.'

Kay gripped her hand. 'Let's hope you're right.'

A hush had fallen over the film set. All eyes were on the Bengali boy as the horses bore down on him.

There was a heart-stopping moment when the angle of the carriage and horses momentarily obscured him and Laura thought he'd been trampled underfoot. Then something incredible happened. The carriage slowed and came to an abrupt, jerky halt. When the horses came into view once more, they were being led by Tariq. A hand waved weakly from the carriage window.

William Raven had survived his ordeal.

A cheer went up. Dozens of people rushed forward to offer their sympathies to the actor and praise Tariq, but a shout from the director stopped them in their tracks.

'If you value your jobs, you will stay where you are until the carriage is safely back on the set, the horses are secured and William is on solid ground. If you surround the carriage, you could start another stampede.'

Laura was dying to rush to Tariq's side, but she didn't dare. As he neared, she could see his lips moving as he talked to the animals, soothing them, telling them they were safe. It was only when he reached the set and was able to hand the horses over to Otto and the groom that Laura saw how pale and shaky he was.

She threw her arms around him and gave him a bear hug. 'I'm so proud of you. You're amazing – a total hero.'

'Yes, you are,' agreed Kay. 'If it weren't for you . . . If the horses had reached the main road . . . If—'

Tariq flushed. He hated being made a fuss of. 'It was nothing. Anyone would have done the same.'

'Yes, but you were the only one who did.'

William Raven offered Tariq his hand. 'Thank you, young man. You averted a catastrophe. At the very least you saved me an extended stay in hospital.'

He seemed sincere in his gratitude, but his eyes were icier than ever. Laura wondered how many people would lose their jobs over the incident before the day's end.

Tariq looked uncomfortable, but he shook the actor's hand. 'No problem, Mr Raven. I'm glad I could help.'

Brett Avery came rushing up. 'Help? You didn't just help, you saved the man's life. That's twice in one week that you and Laura Marlin here – or should I say her husky – have inadvertently plucked one of my stars from the jaws of death. I do hope it's nothing more than coincidence that whenever you show up on my set, drama ensues!'

He chuckled. 'Only joking. Seriously, I'm in your debt. The cameraman kept filming throughout so we now have even more Oscar-worthy footage. Don't you agree, William? We owe these kids.'

The actor's white teeth flashed again. 'We do indeed owe them – and I always repay my debts.'

As the men walked away, Laura thought how odd it was that words that were supposedly meant kindly managed to sound so ominous.

IN AN IDEAL WORLD, Laura would have begun her investigation into this latest accident immediately, but she didn't get a chance. Brett Avery used a megaphone to announce that shooting would be suspended for the rest of the day while the set was made safe and measures were taken to ensure that no similar disaster could happen ever again.

'That's the official reason,' remarked Kay. 'The real reason we have the rest of the day off is that William Raven doesn't want to be around when Brett carries out his orders to fire Otto, the animal handler, or the extra who let the chicken escape, or the groom who didn't catch the horses, or . . . you get my drift.'

Laura was horrified. 'But surely Brett isn't going to listen to him and sack all of those people?'

'Of course he isn't. Brett can be a bit hot-headed, but underneath it all he's actually very kind. However, he will have to shuffle the culprits into different positions in order for our star to feel that his wishes are being taken seriously. My only worry is that if we have many more of these . . . incidents, there'll be nobody left in the crew.'

'What incidents?' Laura asked innocently.

Kay could no longer hide her concern. 'All film sets have their share of drama – you know, fires, injuries, rows – but we've had more than our fair share. Coincidence, I'm sure, but for the sake of crew morale we could really do with a few days where everything goes smoothly.'

'Is that what you believe – that it's nothing more than coincidence?' asked Tariq.

She stared at him in surprise. 'What else could it be? I mean, who could have predicted that the chicken would hop out of the crate at that exact moment and scare the horses? It's bad luck – that's all. Now, since you have the afternoon off, how about I arrange a visit for you to the Hermitage Museum?'

'Bad luck? Coincidence? Personally, I don't believe in either of those things, and neither does Matt Walker,' said Laura as they crossed the canal and walked the short distance to the Hermitage.

She lowered her voice so that she couldn't be overheard by Vladimir, their Russian guide, or the motley bunch of film set folk he was escorting to the museum. 'These "incidents", as Kay calls them, could only be caused by someone with detailed knowledge of each day's schedule for filming. How else could they plan each "accident"? We need to find out who that person is, and if there's more than one of them, before someone else gets seriously hurt or worse.'

'What if we can't?'

'We will,' Laura said, with such determination that even Tariq, who thought of his best friend as the kindest person he knew, felt a chill go down his spine.

At that moment they rounded the corner and saw the Hermitage, one of the greatest, and largest, museums on earth and all other thoughts were forgotten. What made it particularly thrilling was that a marching band in bearskin hats was high-stepping across Palace Square, overlooked by an angel on a skyscraping pillar. Laura and Tariq stood beneath her and gazed at the green, gold and white museum.

'Follow me, follow me,' cried Vladimir, a jolly man with an unruly black moustache. Using a combination of charm and brute force, he cleared a path through the tourists cramming the entrance to the museum. A grinning guard waved them through the barriers.

Vladimir puffed up the Jordan staircase, a dazzling stairway of granite, marble and gold. 'Of all the magnificent attractions in St Petersburg, the State Hermitage Museum is among our proudest creations. It was founded in 1764 by Catherine the Great and has been open to the public since 1852. There are over three million works of art in the collection . . .'

'Three million?' exclaimed Laura. 'We could be here for days.'

Vladimir's moustache twitched. 'Only a fraction of which you will see today . . .'

Laura loved art and had been looking forward to seeing the Hermitage as much as Tariq had, but nothing could have prepared her for its epic scale or for its treasures. Vladimir's monologue had them gasping and laughing as he guided them expertly through the four historic buildings that made up the part of the museum open to the public.

Each was more magnificent than the last, although Laura's favourite was the Winter Palace, once the state residence of Russian emperors. She also loved a Van Gogh painting that seemed to move as if a great storm was brewing in it. Tariq was fascinated by the Egyptology section, which had hieroglyphics, mummies and a statue of Pharaoh Amenemhat III, who'd lived 2100 years BC.

They saw frescoes by students of Raphael, and the carriage used for the coronation of Catherine the Great. Tariq, a gifted tapestry artist, was captivated by the religious tapestries, while Laura loved the boldly coloured paintings of Matisse, Gauguin and Kandinsky. Another highlight was Michelangelo's statue of a crouching boy. It was so real that Laura almost expected the boy to stand up and walk away.

By five o'clock they'd been walking for three hours. Laura

could have wept with relief when Vladimir suggested a stop for a hot chocolate and a pastry. Her new boots had given her a blister.

At that time of day, the coffee shop was quiet and they found a table easily. After Vladimir excused himself to talk to a friend, Tariq helped Colin, a skinny extra with a sweet, sleepy face, to drag more chairs across. The group sat together in a slightly awkward circle, lit by an overhead skylight.

Laura stole a glance at the other occupants of the cafe. Ever since Kay had found the playing card, she'd been keeping an eye out for anyone who might be a spy for the Straight As. So far, she'd seen nothing unusual, but it was important to be vigilant.

Her thoughts turned to the issue at hand. Who or what was terrorising the film crew? She was trying to decide how best to bring up the subject of the runaway carriage when Peggy, a curly-headed fifty-three-year-old from Norfolk, did it for her.

'You're the hero of the day, Tariq. What's *your* opinion? Should the police be called in, or is it the Ghostbusters that we need?'

'Excuse me?' stalled Tariq, startled to find himself the centre of attention.

'What I was wondering,' Peggy said loudly, 'is, do you think that criminals are behind this latest "accident" on the film set, or is something supernatural at work?'

She stabbed her pastry with a fork. 'You and Laura have no idea what I'm talking about, do you? Allow me to update you. What happened this morning, with the horses going berserk and nearly dragging William to his death, is the fourth or fifth catastrophe we've seen since filming began. We've had people poisoned, a couple of broken wrists and lost half of our equipment in a crash. And if it wasn't for your husky, Laura, lovely little Ana María might have drowned in Cornwall.'

'People are calling it a *cursed* set,' said Colin in a hushed tone.

Sebastian Wright, a young British actor tipped to be a future star, was amused. He leaned back in his chair and put his hands behind his head. 'You can't seriously believe in all that superstitious hokum?'

Chad MacFarlane looked up from his slice of pizza. 'What are you saying – that you don't believe in curses?'

'I'd sooner believe in Father Christmas and the Tooth Fairy. No, my friend, I deal only in fact. There are two options here. Either some fruit-loop is on a mission to destroy our film, and what possible reason would anyone have for doing that? Or it's down to sheer incompetence on the part of the production team.'

'Maybe they're jokers by nature as well as by name,' said Bob Regis, a retired insurance salesman from Hull. He'd explained to Laura that his wife disliked travel. Working as a 'background artiste' had been his passport to seeing the world.

'Take what happened this morning,' continued Sebastian, paying no attention to him. 'Somebody didn't secure the chickens' crate properly. If I was directing this film, I'd have used a whip to give the horses a proper fright and then we would have been rid of that fool William Raven for good.'

There was a shocked silence.

'That's a terrible thing to say,' Peggy managed at last. 'William can be a bit full of himself, it's true, but surely you're not suggesting you'd like him dead?'

'Oh, come on Peggy, don't be naïve. Everyone on the set wants something bad to happen to the man. I'm the only one honest enough to admit it. He's insufferable.'

Chad said eagerly, 'If something were to happen to old Raven, would Tiger Pictures bring back Jon Ellis-Harding?' Laura and Tariq had discovered that he was the Hollywood star who'd been replaced in the lead role after the film studio went broke.

'That old has-been,' snorted Sebastian. 'We'd have more luck casting Skye in the role. The dog's a better actor.'

'You remind me of someone, Chad,' said Bob Regis. 'It's been plaguing me since we met. Are you by any chance related to Hugo Porter, who starred in that film about the lighthouse keeper?'

Incensed by Sebastian's comments, Chad ignored him. 'How can you say that? Jon Ellis-Harding is one of the greatest actors who ever lived. He's a thousand times better than you are.'

Bob Regis stood up. 'I think I've heard quite enough. If anyone needs me, I'll be in the gift shop.' Laura smiled at him and Tariq shifted his chair, but the others didn't acknowledge his departure.

Laura watched the young men squaring off as if at any moment they might challenge one another to a duel. In a way, it was hardly surprising. They were opposites. Sebastian was a Cambridge graduate from a wealthy

68

family and a rising star, frequently featured on the covers of magazines. In *The Aristocratic Thief*, he'd been cast as an ambitious young artist who is persuaded to use his talents to fake a masterpiece.

Chad, on the other hand, was a runner, one of the lowliest positions on set. Laura had heard several people making fun of him. 'Not the brightest light in the harbour,' one had said.

To judge by appearances, Chad was the one more likely to succeed as a film star. He had dreamy blue eyes, perfectly behaved blond hair, golden skin and the body of an Olympic swimmer. Sebastian, on the other hand, was small and had pale slim limbs, devoid of muscle. His face was dominated by long-lashed, basset-hound eyes.

Yet Kay had explained to Laura and Tariq that they were mistaken if they thought that any talent scout worth his salt would choose Chad over Sebastian. The former, she said, looked like ten thousand other wholesome, all-American boys.

'Walk down Sunset Boulevard in Los Angeles and you'll see so many perfect people you'll be convinced they're making them in a factory.'

To be a great actor, she told them, you had to be different. The camera adored Sebastian. On the street he might pass unnoticed, but on film he was a chameleon – as capable of being soulful and romantic as he was of playing a darkly magnetic villain.

'The furthest Chad is ever likely to go in acting is if someone casts him in a cereal commercial, whereas for Sebastian the sky is the limit.'

Sebastian, who was well aware of that, was busy rubbing salt into Chad's wounds. 'At least I'm being paid to actually act in films. I'm not spending my days making rubbish coffee and cleaning up horse poop.'

Chad's fists bunched at his sides. He pushed his chair back, his handsome face twisting in anger. 'You—'

'Have we had a lovely, relaxing break?' asked Vladimir, striding across the cafe towards them, a broad smile on his face. 'Have our feet recovered? Have we enjoyed the pastries? Very fine, are they not? Good. Then you are ready for a special treat. I am taking you to see what is arguably the most special painting in the Hermitage. For centuries it was feared lost. When it was found, the whole art world wept with happiness. It is a masterpiece, its worth beyond price. Mere money cannot convey how precious it is, how unique, how profound, how mysterious . . .'

'For goodness sake, man, get to the point,' said Peggy. 'Are you going to show us this painting or not?'

Vladimir looked indignant. 'Or course I am, Madam. But we are talking about art, not groceries. At all times there must be respect. Now, please, come this way.'

~ 9 ~

AFTER VLADIMIR'S BIG build up, Laura's initial response to the painting was one of disappointment. Indeed she was more impressed by the salon in which it was housed, the Leonardo da Vinci Room.

The quality of the light in the gallery and the size of the windows was the first thing that struck her. From the moment she passed through the tortoiseshell veneer and gilded brass-decorated doors, the airiness of the space set it apart from every other section of the Hermitage. Every detail seemed enhanced, as if through a special filter. The lapis-lazuli insets in the marble fireplace were the exquisite blue of Porthminster Beach on a clear day. The ceiling paintings seethed with life.

By contrast, the masterpiece in question, Leonardo da Vinci's 'Madonna and Child with Flowers', famously known as the 'Benois Madonna', was almost dull. Laura stood on tiptoe to try to glimpse it through a gap in the procession of visitors and couldn't understand what the fuss was about.

It was of much more interest to her that the painting was situated right beside a window with no security bars on it – a partially ajar window overlooking the Neva River. She supposed that the picture was alarmed and that there were guards patrolling the halls who would spring into action if anyone tried to snatch it, but it seemed quite vulnerable. However, Vladimir assured her that the Hermitage was impregnable.

'Through the centuries, there has only once been thieves here and they were insiders, working for the museum. They stole some bits and pieces – some ceramics and little statues and such like – over many months. Believe me when I tell you that their punishment has served as a deterrent to others.'

Stifling a yawn, Laura bent down to loosen her bootlaces. She was debating whether to limp across to the 'Madonna Litta' when an elderly man caught her attention. He was sitting on a bench clutching the wooden handle of a mop. Laura had the impression that, without it, he'd collapse at the waist. His head wobbled constantly like one of those nodding dogs in car windows. His face was as wizened as a peanut but he grinned aimlessly and toothlessly at everyone who passed. He seemed far too ancient to be employed as a cleaner, and yet by all appearances that was what he was.

'That's Igor,' said Vladimir, coming over to check on her. 'He is senile and rarely speaks, but he once scribbled his name on some paper. Because he is so decrepit, the museum staff found it quite amusing that his name means Warrior. They can be a bit like naughty children sometimes. They make up stories about Igor's past, each more funny and fantastical than the last.'

'He doesn't have a family?'

'Not that we know of. He appeared about a year ago – a starving street person. He was always sweeping and trying to clean windows in a desperate attempt to make a few roubles. The police kept chasing him off, but winter came and the director of the Hermitage felt sorry for him. He gave Igor small jobs cleaning some basement rooms. To everyone's surprise, Igor turned out to be quite competent and reliable. Eventually, he was given responsibility for washing or polishing the floors throughout the museum.'

He lifted a hand to Igor, 'Good day, my friend,' he said in Russian.

Igor beamed and bobbed his head enthusiastically.

To Laura, Vladimir murmured, 'He is fixated with this room. Museum staff often find him sitting here with tears in his eyes. They believe that the paintings of the Madonna and Child – there are two, as you can see, the 'Benois Madonna' and the 'Madonna Litta' – perhaps remind him of the family he has lost.'

'He's lost his family?' As an orphan, Laura felt great compassion for anyone who was alone in the world.

'We might never know. He can't exactly tell us. He arrived on the wind and he may leave the same way.'

Vladimir gestured towards the 'Benois Madonna'. 'Now, I see you were not very taken with our special painting. Might I have the privilege of explaining to you why it is one of the greatest works of art the world has ever known? It is thought it was the very first painting Leonardo completed on his own in 1478. It was believed to be lost for centuries before it was exhibited in Russia in 1909 by the architect Leon Benois, causing a sensation. Even now mystery surrounds it – no one knows for sure whether it is definitely the work of Leonardo, or if it's even finished.'

As he steered her towards the painting, Laura glanced back at Igor. A family with a boisterous toddler passed him, gabbling loudly. The child was wailing for sweets. In a desperate bid to snatch them from his mother's bag, he tripped over Igor's mop.

The old man's hand shot out so fast that Laura registered it only as a blur. He grabbed the toddler's arm and stopped him from falling flat on his face. The child's mouth opened in a shocked O. His mum and dad were noisily discussing a painting and didn't notice until their son, back on his feet and frightened, let out a piercing screech. Embarrassed, they scooped him up and left the room in a hurry.

Igor heaved himself to his feet. Listlessly, he headed for the door with his mop. No one but Laura noticed him go. All of a sudden the meaning of his name – Warrior – didn't seem quite so funny. Whatever the story of his past, she had a feeling that the museum staff hadn't come close to guessing it.

'You may think you've seen all the treasures the Hermitage could offer, but I have one more surprise for you,' said Vladimir.

Peggy groaned. 'Oh no you don't. I'm bowing out. I've loved every minute but my feet feel as if they've been through a mincing machine.'

'I'm with you on that,' agreed Bob. 'Amazing experience, but another surprise would put me in A&E.'

Vladimir was dismayed. 'But you don't even know what I am going to show you. This will be the icing on the cake of your year. It will be a once in a lifetime experience – a story to tell your grandchildren. It will—'

'Sorry old chap,' interrupted Sebastian. 'It's been a blast, but it's time for some dinner and a stiff vodka. I'll bid you das-vee-DAN-ee-yah. Isn't that the Russian word for goodbye?' He looked pointedly at Chad. 'Besides, I have lines to learn.'

The American boy scowled. 'Thanks, Vlad, but some of us have real work to do.'

Vladimir seemed so crushed that Laura didn't have the heart to tell him that she, too, was desperate to get back to the hotel and attend to her blisters.

'Tariq and I would love to see your surprise, whatever it is,' she told him.

Tariq gave the best smile he could manage. He'd landed awkwardly while leaping from the moving barge that morning and after four hours of walking his knee was killing him. 'Definitely. Sounds great.'

'Young, enquiring minds,' Vladimir said triumphantly to the departing group. 'What could be better? This is the most satisfying part of my job.'

Peggy waved him away with a weary hand and in another minute they were alone.

Vladimir beamed. 'I am so delighted you decided to stay. I promise you won't be disappointed. Follow me.'

Laura and Tariq might have had enquiring young minds, but after the rigours of the day their bodies felt at least a decade older. Clutching each other for support, they limped after their inexhaustible guide. Mercifully, a lift hidden behind a velvet curtain whisked them down to the basement, saving them a trek down the stairs.

The basement had nothing of the grandeur of the museum upstairs. It was shabby and poorly ventilated, with wooden floors that could have done with a polish. At one point a reinforced steel door swung open to reveal a storeroom stacked from floor to ceiling with rolls of canvas and statues swathed in linen sheets.

A hunched man with wild grey hair glanced up to see them staring and slammed the door in their faces.

'It is nothing personal,' Vladimir told them. 'There are riches in that room that could rival the Bank of England. It's his responsibility to keep them safe.'

They came to a locked door. Their guide suddenly became deadly serious. 'Can you keep a secret?'

Laura almost laughed – it was a bit cloak and dagger. 'Of course we can. Why, what are you going to show us – another lost masterpiece?'

Tariq grinned. 'Maybe it's the old headquarters of the KGB spy network.'

Vladimir threw up his hands in disgust. He stalked away down the corridor. 'Nothing. I will show you nothing. Come, let's go. Even though you are only children, I thought you were different. I trusted you. I—'

They limped after him.

'Vladimir, we're sorry,' said Laura. 'Please forgive us. We're tired. That's what we do when we're tired – make jokes.'

'I apologise too,' added Tariq. 'Whatever it is you'd like to show us, we're really interested. Don't worry. We're good at keeping secrets.'

Vladimir took quite a lot of persuading, but eventually he relented. 'Okay, I show you, but be aware that nothing you see here can be revealed outside of this room. If your friends from the film set had come along, they too would have been privy to it. Since they are not . . .' He shrugged. 'How do you say it in English? They are outside the circle of trust. Understand?'

They nodded eagerly.

Vladimir typed a code into a wall panel. The door opened, releasing a pungent odour of oil paints, canvas and turpentine. It was a smell that Laura associated with the artists' studios of St Ives and she felt a wave of homesickness.

The room was a cluttered sea of half-finished canvases,

oozing tubes of paint and used brushes. In the midst of them, a young man with masses of curly black hair was bent over a canvas. He was painting the mane of a chestnut horse with a brush as fine as a cat's whisker.

When he saw Laura and Tariq, he spat a volley of Russian at Vladimir. Reassured by the response, he resumed his task and paid them no further attention.

The guide led them to a canvas draped with a white sheet. When he lifted it, Tariq gasped. 'The 'Benois Madonna'! But we've just seen it upstairs. How did it get here so quickly? Is it a copy?'

Vladimir laughed. 'It is a fake, yes, but you've only guessed that because it is not ten minutes since you saw the original. This painting would fool many of the world's greatest art experts. The artist, Ricardo, who like Leonardo da Vinci is an Italian, is a genius.'

He held up a hand. 'Don't get me wrong. Ricardo is not in the business of faking great paintings in order to deceive or to put money into the hands of thieves. He uses his gift only for good – to restore damaged masterpieces or provide near-perfect copies of the works of the masters as a record in case they are ever ruined by fire or accident or age.'

Tariq leaned closer to the painting. 'It looks a perfect match. It even seems old and a bit faded, like the one upstairs.'

'That is part of Ricardo's brilliance. He uses techniques so sophisticated that they have fooled numerous experts in carbon dating. That's the process used to calculate the age of a painting. We are fortunate that he has chosen to work *with* the Hermitage and not against us.'

Laura studied the picture. Straining to catch a glimpse of it between the jostling tourists earlier, its beauty had been lost on her. It was only now that she saw that Leonardo's (or in this case Ricardo's) use of line and light in depicting the Virgin Mary cradling her child gave the painting an ethereal quality that was almost spiritual. It had an atmosphere. She felt as if she were looking through the window of history at a real life scene.

'This is fascinating, but is there a particular reason why you've brought us here?'

'Because, Laura, this painting is the subject of the movie you are working on. Don't you remember how in the story a priceless picture is stolen by a gentleman thief? For obvious reasons, the Hermitage would not give the film company permission to shoot the stealing of Leonardo's actual painting. Instead the museum recommended that Brett Avery commission Ricardo to make an exact replica. He is expensive, but as you can see he is worth every rouble he has been paid. The director is delighted with the result. I think that is why he has given me permission to show a small number of people the finished picture.'

Tariq was amazed. 'To me, the paintings look identical. How do you tell them apart?'

Vladimir laughed. 'It is impossible to tell with the naked eye. That is how talented Ricardo is. His attention to detail is second to none. Come, watch him paint this horse's mane. He gives it the quality of silk.'

Laura stayed looking at the 'Benois Madonna'. Acccording to the guide not everyone was convinced that it was the work of Leonardo. Some experts believed that, even if it was, it appeared to be unfinished. To her, that only added to its mystique. It also had a sumptuously creamy texture that begged to be stroked.

Impulsively, she touched it.

It was wet. Jerking back, she shoved her guilty fingers into the pocket of her jeans. There was a tiny smear on a flower in the painting. It was so miniscule that it was doubtful anyone would detect it, but to Laura, now feeling sick to her stomach, it was glaringly obvious. Ricardo would surely spot it and tell Vladimir, who'd report her to Brett Avery. Laura would be in disgrace. She'd be fired and put on the next plane back to London.

'Everything all right?' Vladimir asked.

'Fantastic!' squeaked Laura. 'I'm having a wonderful time.'

Tariq's eyes met hers. Something told her he'd seen what had happened.

'Thank you for a great afternoon, Vladimir, but we should probably go,' he said. 'We have a long day of filming tomorrow. The sooner we get back to our hotel, the better.'

'The sooner the better,' Laura agreed weakly.

~ 10 ~

'"**HURRY UP AND WAIT**", that's what we call it in the trade,'
said Kay, smothering a yawn. 'You spend hours and hours
doing nothing, bored out of your mind, and then all of a
sudden it's as if someone has lit a fire under the director's
chair. There's frenzied activity and occasional hysteria,
followed by an intensive burst of filming sometimes
lasting only seconds. Then you're back to waiting around
again.'

The screenwriter was sitting cross-legged in an ancient
leather armchair in the draughty storeroom which, for
the duration of the shoot, would be doubling as a space
for the actors and senior crew to hang out in between

takes. It was known as the Green Room. Laura and Tariq were sharing a sofa with no springs, using Skye as a backrest. Piled on a crate in front of them were numerous coffee mugs, water bottles and paper plates strewn with crumbs.

'I can't understand why most actors aren't the size of houses,' Laura said. 'If I had to do this for a living, all I'd do is lie about eating and reading.'

'Because, darling, most of them are on the latest fad diet,' said the costume designer, overhearing her as he sashayed past to the coffee machine. 'If they're not fasting – i.e. starving themselves – they're drinking grapefruit and celery smoothies three times a day, or popping Amazonian jungle pills chased down with miso soup. Trust me when I tell you that you're better off eating cake. Anyway, you'll be pleased to know that I'm here with a message. You and Tariq are required in make-up. Your scene starts shortly.'

'Hurrah,' said Laura, getting up with rather more enthusiasm than she felt. Ever since the disaster with the painting, she'd been convinced that the long arm of the law was going to descend on her at any moment and that she'd be dragged away and either locked up by the authorities or bellowed at by Brett Avery. It was hard to decide which was worse.

Tariq had been no help. For some reason he found the whole thing hilarious.

'I'm not laughing about the fact that you left a fingerprint on a Leonardo da Vinci masterpiece,' he'd protested as she pretended to punch him. 'I'm laughing because your expression after you touched it was priceless. You looked like a kid caught with their hand in the cookie jar.'

'It's the painting that's priceless, not my face, and I'll probably be forced to pay for it,' Laura said in annoyance. 'I don't see what's funny about that.'

'I'm sorry. But firstly, it's not priceless. It's only a copy. Secondly, the smudge is so small you'd need a magnifying glass to find it. Nobody is going to make you pay for anything. They'll never know, for starters. Even if Ricardo were to notice that a flower petal is slightly uneven, he's unlikely to connect it to you. Given the state of his studio, he'll probably think a rat walked across it or something.'

Laura knew that he was right but her conscience gnawed away at her. They were on their way to the wardrobe department with Skye when she suddenly stopped. 'Tariq, I think I should tell Brett Avery what happened and face the music.'

'Laura,' Tariq said gently, 'if you'd done something to the real Leonardo painting or even damaged the fake one in any noticeable way, I'd be the first person to tell you to confess to Ricardo or the museum authorities. But you haven't. I understand that you're upset about it and I feel bad for you, but what you did was an accident. Tell Brett if you really want to, but it's almost guaranteed that the whole thing will blow up out of all proportion. Without even looking at it, Brett will decide that you've ruined his specially commissioned painting and cost him thousands of dollars and he'll go off like a nuclear blast. Our lives won't be worth living.'

The make-up artist poked her head out of her caravan and waved to them. 'Hey guys, I'm ready for you.'

'Thanks, Gloria,' Laura called. 'We'll be right there.'

She started to move, but Tariq held her back. 'Laura, why don't we keep quiet about the painting for a day or two and see what happens? If Ricardo finds the mark and everyone gets angry, I'll say that it was my fault too and we can face the fallout together. If nobody ever says a thing, then it'll be our secret. When we go to see the film at the cinema, we can have a laugh about how you contributed to a Leonardo masterpiece, even if it's only a copy of one.'

Laura felt a weight lift off her shoulders. What Tariq said made sense. There was no point in provoking Brett unnecessarily. It was not good that she'd left her fingerprint on a petal, but it paled beside the more serious issues the director had to worry about, such as the stars of his film falling off cliffs and nearly being dragged to their deaths by runaway horses.

'You're right,' she said. 'Let's do as you say, except for one thing. If Ricardo does notice the damaged petal and it turns out that it's a massive disaster, you are not taking any share of the blame. It's my fault and mine alone. If there's a price to be paid, I'll have to find a way of paying it."

After the drama of the past few days, it was not only Laura and Tariq who appreciated an afternoon without incident. They learned that filming could be fun as well as frustrating and, on occasion, dull.

That afternoon two crowd scenes were being filmed. In the first one, Laura played the daughter of rich parents and had to walk between them in a dress that made her resemble a Christmas tree fairy. She and Tariq, who was dressed as a choirboy, teased each other about who looked more ridiculous.

Still, when the cameras rolled it all felt terribly exciting, especially since they were filming in and around the Church of Our Saviour on Spilled Blood. The cathedral owed its name to one of the bloodiest moments in the city's history: Emperor Alexander II was assassinated on the site after revolutionaries threw a bomb at his carriage.

Despite its violent history, there was a fairytale aspect to the church's gold and candy-striped domes and exquisite mosaics. The extras – Laura refused to call herself a background artiste – spent most of the time milling around in the sunshine. From time to time, the director yelled and everyone jumped to attention while the cameras rolled. Laura felt quite important and actorly as she trotted between her make-believe parents, one of whom was retired insurance salesman, Bob Regis.

'Enjoying yourself?' he asked her, and she suddenly realised that she was.

'I am. How about you? Are you having a good time?'

'Oh, I'm in my element. I'm rarely happier than when I'm in a foreign country making films. I know I'm only a lowly background artiste, but some days I feel as if I'm a proper actor. Tomorrow I actually will be. I have my first ever speaking part. Three quite dramatic lines. I've been practicing them in the mirror.'

Chad went by with a tray loaded with coffees and sandwiches. His handsome face was sullen.

'That's it!' cried Bob. 'I've got it, boy. It's in the eyes. You look uncannily like—'

'Bobby Regis! It *is* you, isn't it?' A woman in a yellow hoop dress was rushing in their direction, trying not to trip over her petticoat. 'It's Evie Shore. Don't you remember? We did that Romanian vampire movie together.'

Laura left them to their reunion and went to find Tariq. He was having his hair waxed for the next scene. When he glanced up and saw her, he grinned sheepishly, knowing she'd tease him later.

Both he and Laura had been repeatedly told that, while hundreds of hours of film were shot, only a couple were used. There was a strong likelihood that their fleeting appearances would end up on the cutting room floor.

'Who cares. We're here, aren't we?' Laura said to Tariq. 'We're in St Petersburg and we're experiencing another culture and seeing great art and creating memories. That's all that matters.'

Her friend agreed. He was overjoyed to be with Laura and in exotic St Petersburg, but he'd not lost his suspicion of the entertainment business.

'It is all that matters. Who cares if no one ever sees us on the big screen. Fame is overrated anyway. All it means is that people take photographs of you in your swimming costume when you're looking really fat and put them on the front covers of magazines. I think I'd rather be poor and obscure.'

By the day's end, they were so tired they were ready to drop. The second crowd scene, in which they played grubby urchins piling fruit onto a market stall, had gone on for ever. Skye had also been kept busy. His stomach was rumbling.

As they walked through the lobby of their hotel with Kay, Laura's phone rang.

'Hi, Uncle Calvin,' she said, handing Skye's lead to Tariq. 'How's it going in London?'

'It's given me a new appreciation of St Ives. Everyone is so grumpy here and they all behave as if life is a competition or a race. They sprint up and down the escalators on the Underground, throwing back lattes and gobbling breakfast, lunch and dinner on the run. I admit that I'm a workaholic, but these people make me look positively laid-back. How's it going in sunny St Petersburg?'

'Oh, you know, it's non-stop glamour,' Laura joked. 'We're getting the red carpet treatment all the way. Limousines, banquets, five-star catering . . .'

Her uncle laughed. 'Yes, I can imagine. Well, as long as they're treating you well and you're having fun.'

'We're having lots of fun. Yesterday, we spent the whole afternoon in the Hermitage.' She didn't add that the reason they'd been given time off to visit the museum was that William Raven had almost been killed in an on-set accident. There was no point in worrying him unnecessarily.

There was an audible groan on the other end of the line. 'Don't talk to me about the Hermitage. I've spent the last forty-eight hours trying to reschedule Ed Lucas' state visit to Moscow after he decided that he wanted to do a side trip to St Petersburg to see some art. Our security team in Russia has been having a nightmare trying to keep him safe over there. Anyone would think that he actively wanted to get into trouble.'

Laura's opinion of the Deputy Prime Minister took a further dip. He seemed a thoroughly obstinate, egotistical and inconsiderate man. With people like him running the United Kingdom, it was hardly surprising that the newspapers were always complaining about the country being in a mess.

Even so, it intrigued her that any politician would so blatantly flirt with disaster. 'The film set is only a block or two from the Hermitage,' she said. 'Maybe we'll get to see him.'

'I'm relieved to say you won't,' was her uncle's frank response. 'We've arranged for him to have a closed visit. I can't tell you when it is for security reasons, but I can tell you that it won't be on the same day as the film company do their shoot there. I made sure of that. The only public appearance Mr Lucas is likely to make will be at the ballet tomorrow night. That, too, is top secret. Not a word about any of this to anyone.'

'Of course not,' said Laura, crossing her fingers behind

her back. She and Tariq told each other everything and Mr Lucas' St Petersburg trip would be no exception. 'But I do think it's a shame that the Deputy Prime Minister is going to be in St Petersburg and I'm not going to see him. I'm quite curious.'

'Laura, trust me when I tell you that it's a good thing you're not going to get to see him. Keep it that way. We've had so many nightmares arranging his visit that we've codenamed it Operation Misadventure.'

Tariq caught her eye and rubbed his stomach. Kay was talking to a colleague on the other side of the lobby. Laura grinned. 'I have to go, Uncle Calvin. This acting business is hard work and we're starving.'

As she clicked off her phone, Kay came over. 'Ready for dinner, superstars? I know I am. Let's go out and celebrate a day where absolutely nothing went wrong. In fact, everything went right. Smooth as silk. And to top it all, I have some thrilling news. Just remember, you heard it here first.'

'What is it?' asked Tariq, trying to hang on to Skye who'd spotted a waiter with a tray of food.

Kay lowered her voice, 'You may have read in the papers that the Deputy Prime Minister of Britain has been on a state visit to Moscow while we've been in St Petersburg.'

'I did hear something about that,' Laura said vaguely.

'Well, it now turns out that he's going to be coming to St Petersburg! Apparently he's always had ambitions to see the Hermitage.'

Laura resisted the urge to say that she already knew that and had heard it from a member of the inner circle of his security team, the man responsible for plotting every last detail of Ed Lucas' Russian tour.

Except, it turned out, for one unscheduled stop.

'Edward Lucas has another ambition too,' Kay reported triumphantly as they headed across to the lift. 'Brett Avery has just received a personal phone call from him. Your Deputy PM wants to visit the set of *The Aristocratic Thief* tomorrow. Isn't that fabulous? We couldn't hope to buy that kind of publicity. More amazingly still, he's agreed to host the reception we're giving at the Hermitage the night after tomorrow.'

Laura took the opportunity to press the lift button so that her face didn't give away her shock. 'How cool. I hope I get to see him.'

She felt guilty even as the words left her mouth, because it was obvious that this latest detour would be yet another headache for Calvin Redfern. She planned to text her uncle with the information as soon as she returned to the room. Clearly, he hadn't been informed about it or he'd have mentioned it on the phone.

It was only as the lift doors closed and the party was whisked upwards that it occurred to Laura that the malicious prankster who'd been causing mayhem on the film set had yet to be caught. If it was attention that he or she was seeking, there could be no better time to stage an attack than during a visit from one of the world's most high profile politicians.

And what about the Straight As? She hadn't forgotten the Joker in her hotel room. They were a gang who liked to broadcast their misdeeds from the rooftops. It would be typical of them if they chose the visit of a British statesman to a film set in Russia to do something audacious.

There was also the mafia to consider or perhaps a lone assassin . . .

But no, her imagination was running away with her again. Operation Misadventure was only a codename, not a prediction.

AT BREAKFAST LAURA managed to spill half a cup of coffee down the front of her jumper and had to run upstairs to change while Kay, Tariq and Skye waited for her in the lobby. It took her three outfit trials to decide that her pink checked shirt was the only other thing suitable for meeting a visiting head of state. She was rushing to rejoin her friends when her eye was caught by something on the housekeeping trolley parked in the corridor. In among the miniature bars of soap and bottles of shampoo was a deck of cards. The empty box that had contained them lay beside it.

Laura stopped dead. The door beside the trolley was

92

open and a vacuum cleaner was being tugged around the corner of an unmade bed. As if in a dream, Laura picked up the cards. She'd have known the design on them anywhere. The Straight As had left her a Joker with that same intricate blue and red pattern on the back in at least three other locations over the past few months. Each time it had been a warning from the gang and each time it had spelled disaster.

Further along the corridor a door opened and an empty breakfast tray was shoved out. The door slammed shut. Laura fanned through the deck of cards. She was half afraid that all fifty-two of them would be Jokers, but it was a perfectly ordinary mixed pack. If housekeeping were doling them out, it must have been pure coincidence that Kay received the Joker.

The vacuum cleaner was switched off. Before she could move, the maid appeared in the doorway. Her smile changed to a frown when she saw Laura with the cards. Laura put them down quickly.

'I'm sorry. I was just looking. I . . . I don't suppose you happen to know where these cards came from?'

The maid shook her head. 'No English.'

Laura tapped the cards. 'Do you have any more of these?'

'Ah, you take. Yes, yes, you take.'

'No . . . umm, where does the hotel buy them? If I wanted more, where could I get them?' To prompt her, Laura picked up the empty box and pointed to a label saying Made in China.

The maid smiled with relief. She flung open a side compartment in the trolley and gestured inside. Stacked neatly were at least forty identical boxes of cards.

As soon as she stepped into the lobby, Laura was pounced on by Tariq. Kay was near the reception desk talking animatedly on her mobile.

'Where on earth have you been? Kay thought she'd have to send out a search party. She's on the phone to Otto, who is beside himself because Skye is needed in about five minutes.'

'Sorry, I had to investigate something. You know how I was fretting that the Joker card Kay found in our room was a warning to me and that the Straight As were planning some awful crime? Well, we don't have to worry about them any longer. They're not following us in St Petersburg. I was mistaken.'

'How do you know?'

Laura was briefly explaining her rather humiliating discovery that the cards, far from being unique, were actually made in China and widely available, when Kay came running up.

'Good grief, Laura, what were you doing up there – consulting a fashion designer? Otto is having a nervous breakdown. The Deputy Prime Minister is due on set at any moment. I thought you were keen to try to see him.'

'I am. Sorry I took so long upstairs. I couldn't decide what to wear.' She tried not to think about the text she'd received from her uncle that morning about the politician's visit.

L – *unlikely that you and Mr Misadventure will cross paths (he prefers big stars) but if it happens stay well away. Fanatics target people like him all the time and I don't want you and T anywhere near if something goes wrong. CRxx*

'Great,' said Kay. 'Does that mean we're finally ready?'
Laura glanced at Tariq. 'We're ready.'

The film unit had relocated to Palace Square beside the Hermitage, where anticipation levels had reached fever pitch. Gone was the relaxed, lackadaisical vibe that had punctuated the short bursts of filming the previous day. There were no actors lolling half asleep on sofas, or extras playing video games and drinking cappuccinos while in period costume. Instead they rushed about in a state of high anxiety on a set so scrubbed and organised it was almost unrecognisable. Russian policemen in bear fur hats patrolled the fringes.

Everyone not essential to that morning's filming had been banished for the duration of Ed Lucas' visit. Laura and Tariq had been told in no uncertain terms that they were to help Otto with Skye and the horses and leave as soon as they were done.

'You can forget meeting Edward Lucas,' Jeffrey, the production manager, said snootily. 'Only Brett Avery and the stars will be getting to do that. Not the likes of you.'

The door of the trailer behind them opened. Sebastian exited with feline grace. He was dressed to kill in a dark blue suit and waistcoat with fancy embroidery around the edges. Scowling at the production manager's receding back, he said, 'Why does everyone fawn all over William as if he's a superstar, that's what I'd like to know. I'll admit that he's a good actor, but everyone treats him as if he's the greatest talent since Brando. How he got this job I'll never understand. Previously, he was a washed up magician. Scratch the surface and you'll probably find there's nepotism involved.'

'What's nepotism?' asked Tariq. 'Sounds like a disease.'

'It sort of is. Essentially, it's when a relative or a family friend or connection gets you a job you would never have got otherwise and probably don't deserve.'

'You don't think he deserves his role?' pressed Laura.

'No comment. But if I were him, I'd be checking that the gun being used in the next scene is loaded with blanks, not real bullets. In a short space of time, he's managed to make a record number of enemies.'

Chad came striding up in a T-shirt and ripped jeans. 'You're wanted in make-up,' he told Sebastian. 'Hope they have enough of it.'

'Jealousy will get you nowhere. As I've just been telling Tariq and Laura here, connections are what count in this business.'

'Yeah, well, I wouldn't know anything about that,' growled Chad. 'Not having a rich daddy to buy me into films.'

Sebastian's laughter floated back to them as he walked away. He turned to say teasingly, 'Even if you did, MacFarlane, your daddy couldn't afford the price he'd have to pay. Looks aren't everything, you know. By the way, what are you wearing? Are you aware that we have a British head of state coming to see us?'

Chad waited until Sebastian had moved away before muttering, 'One of these days, someone is going to lose patience with that guy and he'll get what's coming to him.'

He spotted Bob Regis emerging from the wardrobe department trailer in a frock coat, breeches and boots. 'Hey Bob, I have a spare coffee and croissant on my tray. Interested?'

'Sebastian criticises William Raven for being full of himself and making enemies, but he's not doing too badly himself,' remarked Tariq as he and Laura walked over to the temporary stables.

'No, he's not,' agreed Laura. 'It's a good thing that the Straight As haven't followed us to Russia. We have enough on our plate trying to figure out who among the actors and crew might actually be a threat and who is simply full of hot air. Let's hope we do it before it's too late.'

~ 12 ~

AT 10.45 A.M. THERE was still no sign of the Deputy Prime Minister and his entourage. Brett Avery, who had delayed shooting a chase scene for nearly two hours in order to have something 'cool' to show his special guest, was ready to burst a blood vessel.

'Can't we call his people?' suggested Kay.

'His people? Are you mad? I wouldn't know where to begin to find them. You don't *call* Ed Lucas. He calls you. No, we have no choice but to start filming now, while the light is perfect, and hope that he comes before we get the last take in the bag. Actors and crew to their stations, please.'

Laura and Tariq crouched unnoticed in a space between two trailers. In the fuss over the missing Deputy PM they'd been forgotten.

Bob Regis passed them on the way to his mark. He caught sight of them and reacted with comical astonishment, doing a double take and putting his finger to his lips. 'Naughty, naughty,' he scolded, bending to their level. 'But don't worry, I shan't tell a shoal. Soul, I mean. I won't tell a shoal. I mean, soul. Oh, whatever.'

He straightened up and marched away like a soldier on parade.

Tariq watched him go. 'Is he all right? He seems drunk.'

'Mmm, I thought so too, but he can't be because I saw Chad taking him a coffee only about an hour ago and he seemed fine then. Anyway, he doesn't seem the type. He was really looking forward to saying his three lines in the next scene. Maybe he's just fooling around.'

'Action!' yelled the director.

Laura forgot about Bob and stood on tiptoes to watch the scene, not wanting to miss a thing. This was Skye's big moment and she was both excited and nervous. It was the part in the story where Violet the orphan realises that Oscar de Havier has stolen a priceless painting. Unable to follow him on foot, she gives chase on a sledge with wheels pulled by her husky. Since a gun would be used in the scene, Otto had devoted time the previous afternoon to getting Skye accustomed to loud bangs.

The cameras rolled and William Raven – or at least his character, Oscar – came running out of the Hermitage, black coat flapping. He fled across Palace Square in the direction of the river. Sebastian emerged next and ran after him. Moments later Ana María, playing the orphan Violet, raced out of the museum and whistled. Skye, who had been waiting for her in a side alley, bounded forward. Violet jumped on the back of the sledge and shook the reins.

'Go, Flash!' she cried. 'Everything depends on you now. Run for your life, boy, run!'

For Laura, it was hard to watch Skye respond to the commands of another girl, but another part of her was thrilled that her husky's cleverness would be captured on film for the world to see. She and Tariq knew how beautiful and brave he was, but it was nice to know that other people would experience it.

With the crew engrossed in the action, the children crept closer in order to get a better view. Only Tariq noticed that a short, pudgy man immediately moved into the space they'd vacated between the trailers.

Oscar de Havier had commandeered a horse and was shooting over his shoulder. In the pursuing sledge, Violet ducked. As the shots continued to ring out, she pulled up her husky, Flash, not wanting to risk his life. They'd caught up to Sebastian, who used the opportunity to jump aboard and use the sledge as a shield.

Bob Regis had explained to Laura that that was his signal to step forward and shout, 'After 'im, Miss! Don't let 'im get away with it. I reckon your dog can take care of himself.'

He got as far as saying, 'After 'im, Mish! Don't let . . .' and then a shot rang out. His body gave an unnatural jerk and he pitched forward and lay still. A trickle of blood ran from his temple and smeared the cobbles.

The film set curse had struck again.

For a couple of seconds, nobody moved. Half the company assumed that the shooting of Bob was in the script. The others were too stunned to move.

The silence was pierced by Ana María's screams. Otto, the animal handler, rushed to grab Skye.

Ana María's mother burst through the ranks of camera crew and lighting operators and flung her arms around her daughter, crying hysterically. Anyone would have thought that it was Ana María who'd been shot, not Bob. Between sobs, she shook a fist at William Raven. The actor had climbed down from his horse and was staring at the gun in his hand as if he had no idea how it had got there.

'You nasty man,' she cried. 'You're mean and nasty to everyone and now finally you kill someone. You go to jail where you belong.'

William Raven was grey with shock. He lowered the revolver to the ground and put both hands in the air as if he were already under arrest. 'It wasn't me. I mean, it was, but it wasn't, I can promise you that. Who loaded the gun?'

'I did,' said the stunt coordinator who'd been brought in to replace Andre March. He looked as shaken as Andre had when he came to see Laura in St Ives. 'But it's been under lock and key the whole time and I double-checked that the bullets were blank before I handed it to Mr Raven. Either he switched them or someone else did.'

'Don't be a fool,' the actor snapped furiously. 'Are you suggesting that I deliberately tried to murder the man? What possible reason would I have for doing that?'

Sebastian looked at him with dislike. 'You might have been aiming for someone different. Me, for example.'

Brett Avery recovered his powers of speech. 'Sebastian, get over yourself. Your ego is getting out of control. Has anyone checked whether poor Regis is really dead?'

The production manager crouched down and felt Bob's pulse. 'If he was any deader, he'd be extinct.'

'Well, that's compassionate, Jeffrey,' said Kay. 'What's wrong with you all? Right, I'm calling the police.'

Laura whispered something to Tariq, who nodded and took out his phone. She stepped forward. 'Before you do that, I suggest you take a closer look at Bob.'

'Will somebody get those children out of here,' ranted the director. 'Good grief. As if we don't have enough to deal with.'

Kay moved to stop the security guard who swooped to grab Laura and Tariq. 'Brett, need I remind you that these kids have already helped save the lives of William and Ana María?'

'That's true,' said William.

'Yes, they did,' agreed Ana María, tugging away from her mother's strong grasp. 'What is it, Laura?'

'It's Bob Regis. He's not dead, he's dead drunk.'

'Please tell me you're joking,' said the director.

Everyone started talking at once.

'Don't be ridiculous,' snapped Jeffrey. 'I checked him. He's as dead as last year's Christmas turkey.'

As if on cue, Bob groaned and writhed. The film set medic, who'd been in the production trailer tending to a background artiste who'd collapsed after mistakenly eating a peanut, belatedly rushed to his side.

'I don't believe it,' said William Raven. 'Here I was thinking that the curse of *The Aristocratic Thief* had struck again, only this time I'd be jailed for murder, as Ana María's mother so helpfully suggested. And all the while we're dealing with an extra who can't hold his drink.'

'I guess that this will be the final straw,' said Chad. 'One too many accidents. I suppose the film will be cancelled now. Closed down.'

'What do you think, Brett?' asked Kay. 'Are we going to admit that our film is cursed and give up and go home with our tail between our legs?'

'I can't answer that until I've spoken to the production company, but I don't think they're going to want to hear that something else has gone wrong. At best, I'll be fired. At worst, they'll cancel the movie.'

Tariq handed his phone to Laura. She read the information on the screen – an old newspaper article – and nodded. It was what she'd expected to see.

'Don't you understand, that's exactly what he wants you to do,' she said to Brett and Kay. 'If you quit the film, he wins.'

The screenwriter stared at her. 'What are you talking about? *Who* are you talking about?'

Laura handed her the phone. 'Chad MacFarlane. He's the one who spiked poor Bob's coffee with some drug or other. He's the one who's caused every other so-called accident that's happened on your film set.'

'Liar!' yelled Chad. 'She's lying. She and her friend and their stupid husky, don't you see, they've been ruining everything.'

Kay's faced changed as she read what was written on the screen. She passed the phone to Brett.

'Is this article accurate, Chad?' the director demanded. 'The one in the *Hollywood Chronicle*? Are you the nephew of Jon-Ellis Harding?' Harding was the film legend who'd been booked to play Oscar de Havier before the studio went bust. 'Is that what this is all about – revenge?'

Chad's golden face contorted with rage. 'I don't know what you're talking about. You should be looking at *him*.'

He jabbed a finger in Sebastian's direction. 'He's the one who's always saying that he wishes that William was dead. The coffee I gave to Bob was one I'd made for William that he decided he didn't want. I'd left it on the tray outside Sebastian's trailer while I was fetching the croissants. Maybe Sebastian put something in the coffee in order to set William up to fall off his horse or have an accident with the gun, or something.'

William was startled. 'Is that true, Sebastian?'

'No, of course not! He's obviously out of his mind.'

'So it's not true that you're always wishing I was dead.'

'No! Well, maybe a little bit. Look, I can explain. Chad's jealous, that's all. He's riddled with envy. He wants to be me, walk in my shoes, wear my clothes.'

'Who would want to be in your shoes, you jumped up little nobody?' thundered William. 'Now I wish I had shot you after all.'

'Like you can talk. If it wasn't for your producer friends—'

'Shut up, Sebastian,' Brett Avery said quietly. 'You're really starting to get on my nerves. Chad, have you done what Laura's accusing you of? Did you do it out of revenge or jealousy?'

'You can't be jealous of someone who's stolen your life. You can only pity them and be angry at them.'

Kay went over to him. 'Chad, did your uncle ever promise you a role in *The Aristocratic Thief*?

If she'd punched him in the stomach, she could not have produced more of an effect. He slid to the ground and hugged his knees, rocking slightly. The wail of approaching sirens almost drowned out his next words and Laura and Tariq had to strain to hear him.

'My uncle promised me Sebastian's role. It was going to be my big break. But that wasn't why I did the things I did. I know what you're thinking but I did them because I love my uncle like a father. When the production company went bust and he was told he was no longer wanted for the film, it destroyed him.'

'But we had no choice,' protested Kay. 'Brett and I wanted him for the role. That's why we cast him in the first place. But our new backers were determined that we should have William Raven. I hate to be the one to break this to you, but we're glad they did. William has been fantastic.'

A tear rolled down Chad's cheek. 'But don't you

understand? You've as good as killed my uncle. It's true that he's a legend, but he's getting old now and lots of people think the way Sebastian does, that he's washed up. When he was cast in the role of Oscar de Havier, it gave him a reason to get up in the morning. He put tons of work into researching the role. Then it was snatched away from him with no explanation.'

'Did you not hear what Kay said?' Brett demanded. 'It wasn't our fault. We did try to explain that to him. We also gave him financial compensation – a lot of it.'

Chad ignored him. 'From that day, he changed. He became sadder and sadder. Finally, he ended up in hospital. They couldn't find anything wrong with him. The doctor suggested to me that he might be dying of a broken heart. So I decided I'd get a job on the film, any job, and get it shut down. Stop it happening.'

There was a long silence, broken by the director. 'Chad, I feel sorry for you and I especially feel sorry for your uncle, but your actions could have killed William and Ana María, did put a man in hospital in Cornwall and forced us to leave those crew members with food-poisoning behind in LA, costing them work. You also destroyed thousands of dollars worth of equipment. I'll plead for leniency but I fear a judge might decide it'll take a jail sentence to persuade you to reflect on your actions.'

He nodded to the Russian policemen who had been called by the security guards. As they closed in, Chad kicked and yelled and threatened vengeance. He was borne away at the same time as Bob Regis was carried to a waiting ambulance on a stretcher.

Brett smiled wearily. 'Well, I don't know about anyone else, but I feel as if I've just gone ten rounds with a black belt karate champion. How many of you think that we should admit defeat and quit?'

Nobody stirred.

'How many of you think that we should pick ourselves off the mat, dust ourselves down and make the best movie we can possibly make? Can I have a show of hands?'

A forest of hands went up.

He smiled for the first time that day. 'I guess that's decided then. William and Sebastian, I'm going to have to insist that the two of you shake hands and get over this pettiness.'

The older actor and the young peacock shook hands rather sheepishly. A cheer went up. Brett whooped. 'Well done, boys. Now let's make an Oscar-winning film, people.'

'Aren't you forgetting something, Brett?' asked William.

'Yes, aren't you forgetting something?' demanded Kay.

'Eh? What's that? Oh. *Ohhh.*' The director had the grace to look shamefaced. 'Laura and Tariq, I'm so sorry. If it weren't for you, we'd never have discovered that Chad was the culprit. He'd have continued to terrorise us until he really did bring about disaster and that would have been the end of the film.'

Laura smiled. 'No problem.'

'Glad we could help,' mumbled Tariq.

'I'm curious to know how you worked it out?' asked Kay. 'What made you think it was him?'

'Something Sebastian said about nepotism.'

'Nepo what?' demanded the production manager.

'It's when a family member helps a relative or friend get a job they don't deserve,' explained Tariq.

'It reminded me of the plot of one of my Matt Walker novels,' Laura went on. 'It made me suspect that there might be a reason why Chad was so sensitive to Sebastian's teasing. When Bob collapsed, I was sure. He was getting too close to the truth. He was convinced that Chad was related to a well-known Hollywood actor.'

'No wonder Chad got so uptight when I said his uncle was an old has-been,' remarked Sebastian. 'Which he is. Hardly surprising that he has a fruit-loop for a nephew.'

Brett Avery turned on him. 'Sebastian, if you say one more word that isn't scripted between now and the end of filming, I'll fire you on the spot. Do I make myself clear?'

There was a loud cheer from the rest of the cast and crew.

Sebastian subsided like a pricked balloon. 'Am I allowed—'

'No, you're not. You're not allowed anything. Now get out of my sight.' Brett clutched his head. 'What a morning. The only small mercy is that the Deputy Prime Minister didn't show up.'

The short, pudgy stranger who'd been standing quietly between the trailers stepped forward. 'Oh, but I did. I'm pleased to say that I witnessed the whole drama. Most amusing it was, too. Better than any live theatre I ever paid to see. Bravo.'

~ 13 ~

THE DIRECTOR PRESSED his glasses firmly to the bridge of his nose, as if their positioning had somehow caused him to overlook their famous visitor. He gulped audibly. 'Sir – I mean, Prime Minister . . .'

Kay poked him in the ribs and said under her breath, 'Deputy.'

'*Deputy* Prime Minister. I'm Brett Avery, the director. I don't know what to say. Please accept my humblest apologies. My incompetent security staff did not alert me to your presence, otherwise I would of course . . .'

The politician bowed his head. 'Of course. Please, say no more about it. I especially requested that my tour attract a minimum of fuss. Allow me to introduce myself formally. I'm Ed Lucas.'

William Raven and Ana María Tyler, accompanied by the girl's suddenly cheerful mother and a chastened Sebastian, came forward in a line, displaying a dazzling array of white teeth.

'But how nice to meet you,' gushed Ana María's mother. Her daughter's sulky face momentarily brightened. Sebastian shook hands eagerly, but with the director's words still ringing in his ears he dared not open his mouth.

That left William. 'An honour,' he said in a deep, sonorous tone, as if he was delivering a line out of Shakespeare.

'The pleasure is all mine,' murmured Edward Lucas. As the men shook hands, Laura was surprised to see a look pass between them. From where she stood it was impossible to tell if it was hostile or admiring, but she was certain they'd met before. They knew each other.

Brett Avery lifted his hands in a helpless gesture. 'I'm afraid, Mr Lucas, that you've not seen us at our best. It's been a morning of mishaps.'

The visitor raised an eyebrow. 'Mishaps? I was under the impression that *you* were under the impression that one of your actors had been shot dead. Is that an everyday occurrence?'

'Definitely not, sir, Deputy Prime Minister. It was simply a miscommunication. The production manager wrongly reported that our finest background artiste was deceased when in fact he was perfectly well. That's what led to the confusion.'

'From what I could see, the actor in question was

unconscious and bleeding. Dead drunk. Wasn't that how the young lady over there put it?'

His gaze alighted on Laura, Tariq and Skye, who were in the process of being shooed off the set by the production manager, Jeffrey. Laura was looking over her shoulder at the time, marvelling that such a nondescript little man could rise to a position of such power. When her eyes met Ed Lucas', a strange electrical sensation crawled slowly over her. It was like standing in a magnetic field.

'Laura did use the phrase "dead drunk", but it was inaccurate because Bob Regis hadn't been drinking,' spluttered the director. He was squirming like a schoolboy caught cheating in an exam. 'I don't run that sort of show. The unfortunate man had his coffee spiked.'

But the Deputy PM had lost interest. 'Thank you, Mr Avery, I'll take your word for it. Would you be kind enough to introduce me to the youngsters who discovered that you had a saboteur in your midst?'

'But they're only . . .'

'Yes?'

The director had been about to say that Tariq and Laura were only extras, but thought better of it. 'I'd be delighted to,' he said hastily. 'They're proving to be invaluable members of the cast.'

Jeffrey hid a scowl as he was forced to relinquish Laura and Tariq, whom he'd disliked on sight for no other reason than that he hated all children. To him, every last one of them was a brat, including and especially that precocious monster, Ana María Tyler, who treated him as if he was her own personal skivvy. However, this pair ran a close second. They'd made him look like a fool over the whole Chad business.

'You can leave your hound with me,' he muttered to Laura. 'I'll take it to Otto. I'm sure the Deputy PM doesn't want it slobbering all over him.'

He snatched at the lead and Skye rounded on him, letting out a ferocious snarl.

'I don't think he likes the idea of being dragged away by a stranger,' Laura said coolly. 'Do you?'

There was an explosive laugh. She and Tariq turned to find the Deputy Prime Minister standing less than a metre away from them. He had somehow crossed the set with wizard speed. Brett Avery was hurrying to catch up with him, his expression panicked.

The first thing Laura noted was that Ed Lucas was not a whole lot taller than Tariq, and the second was that the energy that radiated from him increased the closer one got to him.

Jeffrey was reduced to a quivering jelly, especially after the Deputy PM introduced himself as an animal lover first and a politician second. 'I was only . . . I was just . . . I wanted . . .'

'I know,' Ed Lucas said kindly. 'It's much appreciated.'

Then he turned his back and focused on Tariq and Laura. 'As you've probably gathered, I'm the Deputy PM of your country. When I was your age, I found the world of politics intensely boring and I have to say that nothing's changed. I wouldn't blame you in the least if you'd never heard of me before today. You can call me Ed. And you are?'

'Uh, I'm Laura Marlin and this, umm, this is Tariq Ali,'

stammered Laura, conscious that the entire cast and crew were staring at them in astonishment.

The Deputy Prime Minister had the serene smile of a man accustomed to having the world dance to his tune. It was at odds with his watchful brown eyes, which unnerved Laura by looking through her rather than at her, like one of those airport X-ray machines.

'Delighted to make your acquaintance, Tariq. A real pleasure, Laura Marlin. A most unusual surname you have. It might interest you to hear that I have some experience fishing for marlin, and if there's one thing I've learned it's that they're surprisingly elusive.'

His gaze fell on Skye. 'And who have we here?'

Laura tightened her grip on the husky's collar. 'This is my Siberian husky, Skye, but I'm afraid he doesn't like strangers, even if they are animal lovers and in charge of the British Government.'

'He makes up for it in other ways,' Brett Avery said enthusiastically, trying to make amends for earlier blunders. 'The husky, that is. I didn't mean you, sir. You should have seen what he did in St Ives . . .'

He stopped. Ed Lucas had extended a hand towards Skye. With a whine that ended on a sigh, the husky lowered his head. It was hard to say which was more astounding – that the Deputy PM had managed to touch Skye without being snarled at or even bitten or that the husky seemed to be enjoying it. Laura had never seen her dog act so weirdly. It was as if he had been hypnotised.

'Beautiful animal,' said Ed Lucas. 'Radiates intelligence. How did he lose his leg?'

Half of Laura was flattered by his interest in Skye; the other half wished that she'd listened to her uncle's advice and stayed as far from the man as possible. She made a point of not looking at him. She didn't want him hypnotising her.

'There was an accident. He was hit by a car when he was a puppy.'

A smile tweaked Ed Lucas' pale lips. 'Accidents do have a habit of happening, Laura Marlin, especially if you are of a heroic disposition and put yourself in harm's way.'

'If you have a person with a grudge in your midst, they seem to happen anyway,' joked Brett Avery. 'On this set, at least. Although hopefully with Chad's arrest, that's a thing of the past. Now, sir, you might be interested in talking to William Raven, our star, about—'

'I can't think of anything I'd enjoy more, Mr Avery, but if you'll forgive me I do have one more question I'd like to ask of Laura Marlin.'

The director flushed with annoyance. 'Sure, sure. Go ahead.'

'Thank you. Laura, you mentioned that the plot of a Matt Walker detective novel helped you realise that Chad was behind the disasters on the film set. Is this something that interests you, solving mysteries?'

Laura felt like an insect being examined under a microscope. It no longer surprised her that Ed Lucas was the second most powerful man in Britain. He radiated charisma and some quality that made her want to start babbling as if she'd been given a truth serum. It was on the tip of her tongue to tell him that her uncle had once been

Scotland's best and bravest investigator, but she suspected that Ed Lucas would not be pleased to discover that a lowly extra was linked to the intelligence team protecting him.

She covered her hesitation with a smile. 'I like reading mystery novels. My hero is Matt Walker. He's only a character in a book, but to me he's the perfect twenty-first century detective. He's good at dealing with the sort of international criminals and gangs that do evil things in the modern world.'

'Fascinating. Fascinating,' murmured Ed Lucas. 'Yes, I enjoy reading Matt Walker novels myself. They're far-fetched but quite diverting.'

He looked at Tariq. 'And in this world of modern criminals, who do you think will win, Mr Ali?'

'Excuse me?'

'Who will come out on top? The good guys or the bad guys?'

Tariq brushed his black hair from his eyes. 'Whoever's smartest.'

Ed Lucas laughed. 'Clever answer.'

'In the movies, the good guys always win,' interrupted Brett Avery, keen to bring the discussion to a close. 'Everyone loves a hero.'

Laura felt Ed Lucas' strange electricity transfer to the director. 'Yes, everyone loves a hero, don't they?' he said in his soft, firm voice. 'What a shame it is that real life can't be more like the cinema. On the other hand, the conflicting sides of human nature – light versus dark – are what keep things interesting.'

Seizing his chance, Brett Avery said, 'Definitely. That's

certainly true of the cinema. Now, sir, if you'd like to come this way . . .'

Ed Lucas checked his watch. 'Do you know, I appear to have run out of time. Please accept my sincere apologies, Mr Avery. They have me on this ridiculous schedule, you know. It's a curse of high office. However, as we discussed on the phone I would be delighted to host the reception in honour of your film at the Hermitage tomorrow night – provided, of course, that you allow me to watch you shoot a scene or two later. I will also tell my personal assistant to organise personal invitations for Laura and Tariq. So inspiring to talk to such . . . motivated young people.'

He lifted a hand. Bodyguards in dark glasses materialised from the shadows. Laura blinked. The Deputy PM was gone.

14

'**WHAT DO YOU THINK?**' said Laura, doing a twirl. Ordinarily, she loathed dresses and wore nothing besides jeans, boots, sweatshirts and a jacket with a fake fur collar, but it was fun playing dress-up in the clothes that had been loaned to them by the wardrobe department. In her case, that meant a nineteenth-century cherry-red silk bodice and skirt, under which she'd hidden her lace-up boots. The wax she'd applied to her short, pale blonde hair gave her a slightly gothic look.

'You look like a film star,' said Tariq, who was wearing a white silk shirt with a wide blue collar beneath a black suit. 'Actually no, you look more like a musician. There's a folk singer called Laura Marling. You look a bit like her.'

Laura laughed. 'No, I don't. I look a bit ridiculous. But it's sweet of you to say so. You look quite good yourself. A bit like a rock singer from some eighties band but, you know, it sort of suits you.'

'Gee, thanks.'

'You're both ravishing,' said Kay, emerging from the bathroom in a black cocktail dress that was most definitely not old-fashioned. 'Right, are you ready to go?'

Laura shrugged into a black coat, also on loan from the wardrobe department. She kissed Skye goodbye and he lay on her bed with his nose resting on one paw, looking forlorn. 'We'll be back soon, I promise. No parties.'

Before she left the room, she put her phone in the bedside drawer. That way, if her uncle made a last-minute call to ban her from going, she could honestly say that she hadn't received his message.

The previous evening, she'd had a slightly fraught conversation with him about Ed Lucas' visit to the film set. It began when he called to say that one of the Deputy PM's bodyguards had reported that his boss had had a long conversation with a couple of extras.

'He was sure that one was you. Of course, I sent him away with a flea in his ear. I told him that it was obvious he'd confused you with someone else.'

'It's true.'

'It's true that he confused you with someone else?'

'No, it's true that Ed . . . I mean, Mr Misadventure, spoke to me.'

'You're joking?'

'I'm sorry,' Laura said defensively, 'but what was I supposed to do? He made a beeline for me and Tariq and started asking questions about Skye's missing leg and Matt Walker.'

'*Matt Walker*? Why on earth would he ask you about a fictional detective?'

'It's a long story.'

There was a deep sigh. 'Try me.'

'It was because one of the extras was shot.'

'With a gun? In real life?'

'Yes, with a gun in real life, but don't worry, he didn't die. The problem was that everyone thought he was dead and that William Raven had murdered him by mistake while trying to shoot Sebastian. To be honest, it would have been less surprising if Sebastian had killed William.'

'I'm starting to feel unwell. Are you telling me that live ammunition was being used on the set while one of our most prominent politicians was visiting?'

'No, he wasn't there yet. At least, we thought he wasn't. It turned out later that he was there all along, only in secret. But don't panic – Bob, the dead extra, was only drunk. Or drugged. We don't know which.'

A growling noise came down the phone. 'I might commit murder myself. On Brett Avery. He gave me his word that you'd be safe in St Petersburg. "I'll wrap them up in cotton wool" is what he told me.'

Laura tried not to laugh. 'Believe it or not, we've been very well looked after. It wasn't Brett's fault that Chad – he's this runner who had a grudge – turned psychotic. But we weren't in any danger. He only hurt people who'd stolen his uncle's job. Except for Bob, of course, who hadn't done anything.'

'Don't tell me any more. I think I might have a nervous breakdown. Can we return to the original question? How did you end up in conversation with Mr Misadventure?'

'It was me who guessed that Chad was behind all of the supposed accidents, so after he'd been taken away by the police and Bob had gone off in an ambulance, Mr Misadventure asked me if I liked solving mysteries. That's when I said that I liked Matt Walker novels.'

'That's it?'

'Yes, that's it. He did ask Tariq a bit of an odd question. He wanted to know who Tariq thought would come out on top, the good guys or the bad guys. He's quite weird, isn't he? It's hard to imagine how someone like him got to be so important. Maybe it's because he's good at charming people and because he's electrical.'

'Electrical?'

'You must have noticed. There's this strange energy that comes off him. It's not what you'd expect in such a small, dumpy man. It's as if a lightning bolt has somehow ended up in the most unlikely body in the world.'

Calvin Redfern laughed. 'I know what you mean. Oh well, I suppose you satisfied your curiosity and no harm was done. I must say, I can't wait until this assignment is over and Mr Misadventure is back on British soil. Can't wait till you're home safely either. What are you up to tomorrow?'

'We're doing some more filming with Skye in the morning, but then we've been told we have to nap all afternoon so we're not too tired for the reception at the Hermitage in the evening.'

'The one that Ed – our friend – is hosting? No way. I'm not allowing it. Laura, I've told you that it's too risky. As long as he's in Russia, there's a chance that an assassin could strike.'

'Oh please let us go, Uncle Calvin, it's going to be the highlight of our trip. All the stars will be there and we'll be perfectly safe. Kay says there will be lots of interesting people and great food. And afterwards we've been asked to help with the filming in the museum. Please don't stop us from going. I'll be heartbroken.'

Another deep sigh came down the line. 'It's really that important to you?'

'Yes, it is. Anyway, Kay will be there to look after us. She won't let us out of her sight.'

'This Chad character – he's been arrested?'

'Yes, he's under lock and key.'

'All right, you can go. Only Laura . . .'

'Yes?'

'Be careful. Try to remember that you're not in St Ives any more. St Petersburg is a much darker place.'

The lift doors pinged open. Laura followed Kay and Tariq into its fluorescent depths. She thought of Ed Lucas' watchful brown eyes; the way he'd hypnotised Skye and looked through her as he interrogated her. She had the idea that he only asked questions to which he already knew the answers.

'Everything all right, Laura?' asked Kay. 'You seem deep in thought.'

'Everything's fine. I was thinking about tonight. I've a feeling it's going to be unforgettable.'

As they walked through reception, the concierge ran after Kay. 'I thought you had already gone out, Madame. You have just missed a phone call. There is a man who is desperate to get hold of you. He said it's a matter of life and death.'

'Thank you,' said Kay. 'I know who it is and I'll call him later.'

'But . . .'

'It's fine. Really. I'll call him later.'

As they exited through the revolving doors, she said with an eye roll, 'There's this Russian oligarch – an oil trillionaire, in case you didn't know – who thinks he can buy his son a starry career in Hollywood. He's nearly driven me mad over the last few days, calling to see if we can write this boy into the script. I absolutely refuse to allow him to spoil my evening.'

They strolled along the canal, past the pastel painted buildings and cafes offering crêpes. Riverboats packed with jubilant tourists chugged by. The film set had been removed from Palace Square, but the trailers used by William Raven and Ana María Tyler were parked in a side alley, along with the film unit truck containing cameras and lighting equipment.

As they passed it two guards in bear hats moved to let in

a limousine. The electronic gates sighed closed behind it. Four figures climbed out – two bodyguards and the man and woman they shielded.

'The governor of St Petersburg and his wife,' whispered Kay.

As the party moved away into the shadows, Laura saw a gun outlined against the hip of one of the bodyguards. It was a warm evening but she shivered. All along, she'd viewed her uncle's concerns about the possible dangers of Russia as being exaggerated. From what she'd seen since arriving, St Petersburg was a friendly, rather gentile city. Now she realised that was an illusion. It was a beautiful city, but one with a dark heart.

Crossing the shaded courtyard that led to the entrance of the Hermitage, she felt a sudden urge to hear Calvin Redfern's voice. She wanted to reassure him that she was with Kay and Tariq and that he didn't need to worry.

She caught her friend's arm. 'Tariq, I've left my phone at the hotel. Is there any chance I could borrow yours to give my uncle a quick ring?'

The reception guests were filing into the museum in all their finery and both Kay and Tariq stared at her in surprise.

'What, now?' Kay asked. 'Is it something urgent?'

'Sure,' said Tariq, pulling his mobile from his pocket.

Laura was embarrassed. 'I'm sorry. I should have done it earlier. I only wanted to tell him Tariq and I are fine and that I don't want him fretting.'

'You are blocking the way. Are you going in or not?' demanded a man with a stomach so vast it could have seated a party of six. His tuxedo squeaked at the seams.

'I spoke to him first thing this morning,' Kay told her. 'I assured him that this evening would be a lovely treat for you and Tariq. I also told him that he was fussing unnecessarily and in the end he agreed. By the time I put down the phone, he was laughing.'

'You are moving, yes?' boomed the large Russian.

Laura handed the phone back to Tariq and moved forward in the queue. 'You're right. There's not much point in calling now, anyway. London is three hours behind and I don't have any news. I'll text him when we get back to the room and tell him all about the night we got to hang out with the stars.'

15

THE RECEPTION WAS held in the Winter Palace, in a salon illuminated by a chandelier so sparkling it could have been made entirely of diamonds. On one side of the room was a large glass cabinet housing a solid gold pheasant. It surveyed the crowd regally, one claw raised. A single gold feather could have bought and furnished Calvin Redfern's entire house.

On the other side of the room was a small stage, at the top of which was a black screen flanked by two giant vases of flowers and two armed guards. A microphone was being set up by a poker-faced technician.

The room was already packed when they arrived.

Women draped in jewellery so heavy that Laura feared for the health of their necks paraded by on the arms of men who resembled penguins in their tuxedos. Glasses tinkled. A smiling waiter presented Laura and Tariq with a lychee cocktail.

It was 7 p.m. but beyond the velvet drapes that hugged the windows, the summer sun still lit the surface of the Neva River. Laura and Tariq, who'd gone without lunch on the promise of fabulous hors d'oeuvres, stopped every passing waiter and piled their plates high with mini pizzas and quiches and California sushi rolls. There were even tiny ice cream cones for dessert. At one point, a silver bucket heaped with black caviar was offered to them, but they drew the line at that. It smelled foul.

As they ate, they leaned against the windowsill and watched the room. With the exception of Ana María, they were the youngest people there. Much to the disgust of Jeffrey, who had not been invited, they were the only extras.

'It's like seeing an ant colony at work,' commented Tariq. 'Everyone is on a mission to achieve something, but they're all pretending that they're only here to have a good time. Meanwhile, they're desperately trying to network with someone richer or more connected than they are.'

'I'm not sure they're like ants,' said Laura, as she watched William Raven, Sebastian and Ana María's mother move through Russian high society, dispensing charm as if it were chocolate. 'Ants are quite friendly. Sharks would be more accurate.'

As she spoke, there was a commotion. Igor, the ancient cleaner, was trying to enter with his mop. The muscle-bound doormen who, Laura suspected, were either part of Ed Lucas' security detail or Russian ex-Special Forces soldiers, barred his way. When he tried to push past, his grey head nodding, their attempts to dispatch him became firmer. They laughed as he tottered away.

'Do you think we should check if he's all right?' Laura asked Tariq.

'Who's that?' demanded Kay, arriving with two glasses of sparkling elderflower.

'Igor,' Tariq explained. 'He's the old cleaner the museum staff have nicknamed "the Warrior". He's quite decrepit. The security guys were being mean to him.'

'I'll be the worrier if you disappear,' was Kay's retort. 'Laura, your handsome but very stern uncle gave me strict instructions to watch you both like a hawk tonight. I don't know what he thinks is going to happen – the museum is closed to the public and there are more guards than statues in the Hermitage. Nonetheless, you're going to stay right here by my side. Besides, the big event is about to start. You'll be sorry if you miss it.'

The Deputy Prime Minister had been scheduled to make a special presentation at 7.30 p.m., but by 8.05 p.m. he hadn't shown up. Brett Avery, who'd been granted permission for only two hours of shooting at the museum that evening, was becoming more agitated by the moment. Every time he paced past them, a vein popped in his neck.

'Ed Lucas may be a big deal in political circles, but frankly I think he's rather rude,' said Kay. 'I don't care if he's the—'

'Shh!' An elegant woman in a pale turquoise ball gown

glared at her. The chatter in the room cut off so abruptly it was as if a mute button had been pushed. There was a grating noise and an ancient mosaic of a monk detached from the wall and swung open. Through the secret portal stepped the evening's star guest. Cheers and applause greeted his arrival.

Ed Lucas looked slightly more impressive in a black tuxedo and crisp white shirt than he had on the film set in a grey suit. Yet his presence transformed the energy of the room. Everyone snapped to attention. Men looked alive and keen to impress. Women twinkled like candles.

His fluid walk carried him so quickly towards the microphone that, from a distance, he appeared to levitate. He trotted up the steps onto the stage, followed by Ricardo, the artist. They made an incongruous pair – Ricardo with his swarthy skin and wild mop of black curly hair, and Ed Lucas, pale and uninteresting. Yet even when they were joined by the smartly groomed governor of St Petersburg, it was to the Deputy PM that every eye gravitated.

'His eminence, the governor of St Petersburg, ladies and gentleman, boys and girls, let me start by apologising for my late arrival. I hope you will forgive me when you learn that it was because I was overseeing the packaging of some special gifts, which you will receive on your way out. I don't wish to spoil the surprise, but every one of them contains a jewel-encrusted Fabergé egg . . .'

There was a gasp from the crowd.

He grinned. 'Not a real one, I hasten to add . . .'

Lots of laughter.

'I'm honoured to be your host on this wonderful

evening where the great and good have gathered together to celebrate the making of *The Aristocratic Thief*. I don't know about you, ladies and gentlemen, but I love that title. For those of you not familiar with the story, it's about an art heist – a theft. A rich and powerful man steals a painting from one of the greatest treasure houses on earth – the Hermitage. He almost gets away with it, but an orphan girl ruins his plans.'

He shook a finger at the audience in mock warning. 'In case any of the aristocrats here this evening have any ideas of doing something similar, let me assure you that the museum director has tripled the usual security. You'll be dealing with people a lot larger and a whole lot more scary than an orphan girl.'

More laughter.

'Without further ado, I have the privilege of asking William Raven up to the stage to unveil the painting that will be "stolen" from the Hermitage in the film. It is a copy of a Leonardo da Vinci masterpiece, the so-called "Benois Madonna". Ricardo, the artist who took on this project, is a genius himself. I would defy any of you to tell the real painting from the fake, but if you think you can, do let me know.'

William Raven joined him on the stage. Laura watched closely to see if any look passed between the men, as it had done on the film set, but their smiles and handshakes seemed purely professional.

The guards moved the screen that hid the back of the stage. Behind it, propped on easels, were two paintings draped in black cloth.

Ed Lucas beamed up at the actor, who was at least twice his size. 'Would you do the honours, William?'

But as William stepped forward, there was an almighty crash. The waiter carrying the silver bucket of caviar had tripped, sending slimy pellets of fish eggs cascading all over the dresses of the governor's wife, her glamorous daughters and a Russian oil billionaire. The screams that followed were so piercing that Laura was amazed there was a glass left intact.

There were several minutes of bedlam while the mess was sorted out and the angry billionaire and crying women were escorted from the room by the governor and various officials. Laura felt sorriest for the waiter, who would doubtless be fired.

'May I humbly apologise and ask the forgiveness of anyone affected by this unfortunate incident,' said Ed Lucas when the room was finally silent. 'I have promised the governor that I will buy his wife and daughters brand new dresses from a designer of their choice. Of course, it's a promise I may live to regret . . .'

There was relieved laughter.

Once again, Laura marvelled at how effortlessly he won people over with his charm and generosity. She could feel herself warming to him. After all, he had admired Skye.

'Seriously,' he went on, 'it would be my pleasure to make amends. Now if there are no more buckets of caviar to spill, shall we return to the evening's main attraction? William, kindly unveil the paintings.'

The actor swept the cloth from each picture, as if he were a matador twirling his cape. The audience cheered.

'Extraordinary,' marvelled the Deputy Prime Minister, peering closely at the paintings. 'In my opinion, we have two masterpieces here, not just one. But don't take my word for it. If you would be kind enough to form an orderly queue, I'd like to invite you to inspect them at close range. Ricardo will be here to answer any questions. Before I go, I would also like to advise all would-be thieves that the museum knows which painting is the original!'

As he and William left the stage to thunderous applause, they were engulfed by a circle of celebrities.

'Care to see the paintings up close?' Kay asked Laura and Tariq. 'Or are you content with the private view you had on your tour with Vladimir? Of course, you didn't have a chance to compare them. Brett and I were invited to see them side-by-side the day after the copy was completed. To me, they looked identical.'

On the one hand, Laura was curious to see whether her fingerprint was still on the painting, or if it had been noticed and corrected by Ricardo. On the other hand, she still felt guilty about what had happened and was nervous even now of her crime being discovered.

'Once was enough,' she said with feeling.

Tariq caught her eye and smothered a laugh. 'Yes, I feel the same. Besides, we should probably go and find Jeffrey and find out if he has any jobs for us. I'm really looking forward to seeing how you film the theft of the painting.'

Kay smiled. 'So am I, but I can't help feeling that I might be arrested at any moment. I know we've had permission and that the painting we're using is a fake, but it still feels wrong to be filming an art heist at a museum in broad daylight. But I'm being silly. It'll be fun. Tomorrow's shoot will be even more exciting. The submarine we've hired for the getaway scene has arrived and is ready and waiting for us on the river outside. Can't wait to see it.'

'A submarine,' cried Tariq. 'How cool.'

'Kay, honey, there you are,' said Brett Avery, rushing up to them in a state of high agitation. 'I need your help. Ana María's mother is having a fit about her daughter's costume. Says it isn't flattering enough. Would you mind coming to talk to her before I strangle her with my bare hands?'

16

'**DO YOU THINK** anyone will believe us at school when we tell
them what life is really like on a film set?' asked Tariq as
he and Laura followed the director and screenwriter into
the Leonardo da Vinci Room on the first floor.

'No,' said Laura, 'I don't. Even if they did, we should
probably avoid the truth in case they have to spend the
rest of the term in counselling. We could pretend we're
writing a story for a celebrity magazine and give them a
rose-coloured version of events. We could say that William
Raven is sweet and humble, and that Sebastian is not in
the least conceited, and that Ana María's mother never
behaves like a crazy stage parent.'

Tariq laughed. 'She's all right, Mrs Tyler. Any parent would go a bit crazy if they saw their daughter fall off a cliff or appear to be involved in a shooting.'

'That's true,' admitted Laura. 'It's just that—'

'Are you two working tonight or would you prefer to stand around idly chatting?' demanded the production manager. 'Because if it's the latter, I can have you escorted back to the hotel.'

'Would you leave these poor kids alone, Jeffrey?' scolded Kay. 'In between saving the lives of our stars, they do deserve to enjoy themselves occasionally. Are you forgetting that they're here at the invitation of the Deputy Prime Minister of Britain? Speaking of which, would you mind fetching Ed Lucas a chair? He's going to sit beside Brett and watch us film the heist scene.'

At the mention of Ed Lucas' name, the hairs on Laura's arms stood up. She didn't like the idea of another encounter with him, but at the same time she didn't want to miss the shooting of the film's most exciting sequence. She couldn't understand why a man of his position was bothering with something so frivolous. It was only a movie. Surely he had more important concerns. World peace, for example.

Then again, even politicians had to have the occasional break. According to Kay, government ministers rarely cared about, or put money, into the arts and it was a coup to find one who did. Still, it annoyed Laura that the Deputy PM had caused so many problems for her uncle during his time in Russia.

She needn't have worried about meeting Ed Lucas again. He entered the room in a bubble that included the film publicist, one of his bodyguards and sundry hangers-on and was escorted to the chair beside Brett Avery. Laura and Tariq were banished to the far corner of the gallery by Jeffrey, who seized them the moment Kay's back was turned and told them that, in his opinion, children on set should be 'unseen and unheard.'

'I'm not sure you mean what you think you mean,' Laura told him. 'Your grammar is a bit twisted.' But he just glowered at her and repeated his threat about dragginging them back to the hotel if they didn't do as they were told.

They were reprieved when there was a sudden buzz on the set and the production manager had to rush away to deal with a crisis involving a missing camera battery.

Screened from the room by a row of tall equipment cases, Laura and Tariq coiled cables as Jeffrey had instructed and peered through the gaps between the boxes as the crew lit the scene. Ricardo's fake painting had replaced Leonardo's original in the spot beside the window. Most other paintings in the room had been replaced by copies or less valuable pictures in case they were damaged during filming.

Old Igor came nodding and creaking into the gallery with his mop.

'Excuse me,' called Laura. 'I saw what happened downstairs. I mean, with the doormen being horrid to you. Are you okay? Would you like to sit with us and watch the filming?'

His head snapped round like a startled turtle and something unreadable flashed through his eyes. He was mumbling something incoherent when Jeffrey bore down on him.

'No, no, NO! Igor, please, we are about to shoot a scene. You have to leave immediately. When it is over, we would be grateful for your services, but not now.'

As the door shut behind Igor, Brett yelled the now familiar word: 'Action!'

Laura and Tariq had moved the equipment cases slightly so they could see better, but their view of the scene was still slightly blocked by cameras, crew and Brett Avery and Ed Lucas. Laura hoped the Deputy Prime Minister didn't melt in his jacket. The studio lights were so intense that the room was like an oven. It was after 9.30 p.m. but the sun still shone outside.

William Raven, dressed once more as the aristocrat, Oscar de Havier, strolled into the gallery and pretended to be admiring different pictures. When he reached the 'Benois Madonna', he paused to study it. A couple with an unruly child passed him. The boy, aged seven or eight, kept complaining that he was bored. He reminded Laura of the boisterous toddler who'd tripped over Igor's mop, except that he was older.

This boy, spiky-haired and spoilt, upset the gallery guard by touching a statue clearly marked 'DO NOT TOUCH!' Oscar de Havier, still standing near the window, scowled his disapproval. It had little effect on the boy. He continued to whine and fuss. When his mother snapped at him, he reacted by prodding a nearby oil painting, setting off the gallery alarm.

The noise was ear-splitting and brought guards running from all over the gallery. They were on the verge of arresting the boy's parents when the aristocrat intervened. It was not their fault, he explained to the guards. They'd done their level best to keep their boy under control, but he'd been determined to cause trouble. Fortunately, no real harm had been done. However, it might be a good idea for them to leave the gallery before they found themselves trying to come up with the money to repair a Rembrandt or a Da Vinci.

The embarrassed parents were escorted out of the room by the guards. Every other visitor had either fled in panic, or been frightened out of the room by the aggressive guards. The alarm was turned off while the crisis was sorted out.

Eventually, Oscar was left alone in the room. A sly smile came over his face. He opened the window and waved a white handkerchief out of it. A masked figure wearing black came abseiling down from the roof of the Hermitage and landed on the ledge outside. A poster roll was strapped to his back.

Oscar took it from him and removed what was supposed to be the Leonardo copy. Kay had explained to Laura and Tariq that it was actually a blank piece of canvas. They would edit in an image of the copy at a later stage. Oscar had to slice the 'original' from the frame and replace it with the fake. He'd been given a spare frame for this purpose. He then rolled up the 'real' painting and handed it to the masked man on the window ledge. Snatching it, his accomplice dropped out of sight.

As Oscar wrenched shut the window, the door of the gallery burst open. A guard ran in.

'What's going on? I heard a noise.'

'Of course you heard a noise,' the aristocrat replied smoothly. 'The alarm went off. It nearly shredded my eardrums. A brat of a boy took it into his head to poke the Rubens over there.'

'I don't mean the alarm. It was a suspicious sound. A scraping sound, as if a window was being opened.'

'That's because it was. By the time every man and his dog had been in to attend to that horrible boy, it was so stuffy in here I started to feel a bit dizzy. I'm afraid I opened the window to gasp for air. Apologies if it's not allowed.'

'It isn't usually, but since it was you, Mr Havier, there is no problem. Forgive me if I was a bit abrupt. Our nerves are all on edge tonight. We pride ourselves on our ability to keep these treasures safe.'

'Don't mention it, my dear man. I quite understand. Now if you'd excuse me, I must be on my way. Goodnight.'

As he swept from the room, he gave a villainous smile.

'Cut!' cried Brett Avery. He jumped out of his seat. 'Great work, William! What a performance.'

'I agree,' said Ed Lucas, marching forward, hand outstretched. 'I don't know about anyone else, but you had me convinced that you could be a master thief.'

'Thank you, Mr Lucas. That's quite a compliment coming from you.'

'I never thought I would hear myself say this, but that was the perfect take,' interrupted Brett Avery. 'We'll do one more, just to be sure, but I'm delighted with how that went.'

He pushed his glasses up the bridge of his nose. 'Mr Lucas, sir, I owe you a debt of gratitude. Your presence inspired our actors to raise their game. They performed out of their skins.'

'The pleasure is all mine, Mr Avery. I shall remember this night for the rest of my life.'

Laura and Tariq, who'd emerged from behind the equipment cases and were diligently tidying cables so that they could listen without appearing to listen, were taken aback when the Deputy PM approached them.

'What did you think of the scene?' he asked jovially. 'Did you enjoy it? Was it clever enough for you? Or would you or Matt Walker have figured out the plot and put a stop to it?'

He winked. 'Personally, I think you might.'

17

'WHAT WAS THAT all about?' said Tariq as he and Laura walked into the basement room which was a combined hair and make-up studio and storage facility for all cast and crew. 'Why ask a question and then walk away without waiting to hear the answer?'

Laura helped herself to a chocolate biscuit from a plate near the coffee urn.

'Because he enjoys toying with people. It's not personal. According to Matt Walker, that's what politicians do. They're sort of like cats. Occasionally, they'll be nice to other cats, usually because they want something or because the other cat has sharper claws, but most of the time they prefer to play cruel games with creatures much smaller or weaker than they are. It amuses them.'

'What's this about cats and mice?' asked Kay. 'I hope there are no rats in the museum, nibbling at priceless works of art. That would be a catastrophe.'

She picked up a biscuit. 'Did you enjoy the shoot? In my opinion, the second take was better than the first, but Brett disagrees. Ideally, we'd have liked longer to work on the scene, but the museum want us out of here as soon as we're done with the shoot on the main staircase – that's the one where Violet pursues Oscar. Brett is filming it now and I have to join him. You're welcome to come and watch, but it's one of those hurry up and wait scenes. We'll shoot for twenty seconds, then spend twenty minutes setting up again.'

Laura, who had already concluded that the life of an extra was not for her, was unable to conceal her lack of enthusiasm.

Kay smiled. 'I understand completely. Filming days can be long and, for the most part, quite tedious. Don't worry, it'll all be over soon. If you're tired or cold, why not stay here and have a hot chocolate. You'll be quite safe. If the make-up artists don't scare off any would-be assassins . . .'

'We heard that!' called Gloria, a towering blonde woman in red stilettoes.

'See what I mean? If Gloria doesn't frighten any bad people away, the guard will. He's here to keep an eye on the "Benois Madonna" until it's returned to the Leonardo Room shortly.'

It was only then that Laura noticed that beyond the area where the make-up artists and stylists were working, a lone guard watched over the painting. The picture was covered once more with the black cloth.

'Before I go, I have something interesting to tell you,' Kay was saying. 'When Ed Lucas visited the museum earlier today, he noticed that Igor's toes were sticking out of his shoes. He sent one of his lackeys to buy the old boy a pair of top-of-the-range trainers – only black. Presented to the cleaner when we finished shooting after everyone but me had left the Leonardo Room.'

'That's very kind of Ed Lucas,' said Tariq. 'You wouldn't think that a man with that much power would even notice a cleaner.'

'That's what I thought, but Brett told me that he was orphaned when he was a baby and that he apparently comes from very humble beginnings. It's good to know he hasn't forgotten them. Igor was almost beside himself with happiness. He put the shoes on immediately. When I left the gallery, he was cleaning the floor around Ricardo's painting and beaming from ear to ear.'

'Where's Ed Lucas now?' asked Laura.

'Already tucked up in his hotel bed, I expect. He said he was worn out and ready for a long holiday somewhere sunny.'

The new runner – Chad's replacement – came rushing in. 'Kay, Brett needs help with a script change. He says it's urgent.'

Kay picked up her bag. 'Heaven help me. See you shortly, kids.'

'Actually, I think I will come with you, if that's okay,' said Tariq. 'I'm curious to see how they do the scene. Do you mind, Laura?'

Laura took a sip of hot chocolate. 'Not if you don't mind if I stay here and chill. I can talk to Gloria if I'm lonely. Have fun. See you in a bit. Oh, Tariq, can you leave me your phone so I can text my uncle?'

Left to her own devices, Laura ate another biscuit and texted Calvin Redfern to say that the evening had gone off without a hitch and they'd had a great time. *Looking forward to bed tho!* she added. She had just pressed send when the phone started buzzing. It was a call from an unknown number. She didn't answer. If it were Tariq's foster parents, their names would have shown up. It was more likely to be a marketing person in the UK trying to sell double-glazing and if she picked it up Tariq would incur roaming charges.

When her uncle didn't reply, she assumed he was busy working. Ed Lucas was returning to the UK the following day so in all likelihood her uncle was in the midst of top-level security briefings. She wondered if he'd had any problems that evening, or if any Russian mafia had been lurking in the crowd.

It was cold in the basement so she put her coat on over her dress. She was glad that she'd insisted on wearing her boots beneath it instead of the uncomfortable shoes with heels the wardrobe woman had tried to press upon her.

Hopping up, she wandered over to Leonardo's masterpiece. It would be good to see the original close up, without having to peer at it between jostling tourists.

The guard was thrilled to have someone to chat to. He removed the cloth reverently.

'Great piktcha,' he said in heavily accented English. 'You like? Leonardo a very great genius. Thees one of his best walks. *Works.*'

'It's beautiful,' agreed Laura, not altogether sincerely. The painting hadn't grown on her with time. It was a masterful piece of art, but . . .

The thought froze in her brain. Her eye had come to rest on the flower. There was a tiny smear on the blue petal. But no, that couldn't be, because this was the original painting.

She stared at it intently. Her brain must be deceiving her. But the harder she stared, the more obvious the smear became. She couldn't believe that the guard hadn't noticed it. It was like staring at someone with a giant red nose and not mentioning it.

'You like?' he asked again.

'Umm, yes, amazing. Thank you,' Laura said distractedly. As she walked away, leaving the guard frowning behind her, she shoved her hands into the pockets of her coat. She didn't want him to notice them shaking.

'Everything all right, love?' asked Luc, the chief hair stylist, who was packing up his driers and potions. 'You look a bit peaky.'

Laura forced a smile. 'I'm good. It's been a great night, but I think I'm ready for bed.'

'I hear you.'

Laura sat down at the table and took a swallow of her lukewarm hot chocolate. If this painting was the copy, the original must have been the picture used in the filming. Since it hadn't been damaged, it wasn't a big deal, unless . . .

The mug began to shake in her hand. Unless the pictures had been swapped deliberately in order to give someone the opportunity to steal Leonardo's version.

But no, that was ludicrous.

Laura picked up Tariq's phone and checked to see if there was a free Wi-Fi signal. There was, but it was faint. As she waited for a search engine to load, a jumble of images poured into her head.

She remembered how, on her first visit to the Hermitage, Igor, seemingly frail and senile and barely able to carry his mop, had saved the boisterous toddler from falling. His hand had shot out with the speed of a cobra strike.

He arrived on the wind, Vladimir had said, *and he may leave the same way.*

'*Who will come out on top?*' Ed Lucas had asked Tariq. '*The good guys or the bad guys?*'

She thought of the Joker on the hotel bed on the first night – the card she'd dismissed once she'd decided that it was a mere coincidence.

Laura's hands were trembling so much that her fingers were clumsy on the phone's miniature keyboard. Twice, she misspelled the name she was after, hit enter too soon and had to start again. She debated whether or not to call her uncle, but he hadn't replied to her text, which meant he was working. Anyway, it was hard to know what to say. Her uncle's faith in her was touching, but even he would find it hard to credit if she called to say that the Hermitage might have been the target of one of the biggest art heists in history, only she was the only person who'd noticed.

She tried the search engine again, but the page refused to load. The signal in the basement was too weak. There was nothing for it but to take the lift to the first floor and return to the scene of the shoot. That way, she could see for herself if there was anything amiss. If the original was still there – and there was no reason that it shouldn't be – she could simply take Brett or Kay aside and tell them that the painting had been swapped by accident and that they should correct the situation before someone got into trouble.

The hair stylist was making himself a cup of tea when she approached him.

'Luc, if Tariq and Kay come looking for me, would you mind telling them that I'll be back shortly? I'm nipping upstairs to fetch something from the Leonardo da Vinci Room.'

'Sure thing, hon.'

There was no one in the corridor. As the service lift rose with a jerk, Laura's heart slammed painfully against her chest. She checked the phone. Still no signal. No reply from her uncle either.

The lift rocked to a halt and the doors shuddered open. The main lights were off and the corridors and salons were illuminated only by cat's eye lights situated at intervals. It was hard not to feel spooked and Laura had to summon every ounce of courage in order to continue. She considered going back to get Tariq or ask Kay's advice, but that would take five or ten minutes. If someone were intent on stealing the painting, every second counted.

Heart thumping, she set off in the direction of the Leonardo da Vinci Room. The ghosts of the dead Tsars and the eyes in the paintings seemed to follow her. For one horrible moment, she envisioned the film company leaving the Hermitage without her. She'd be trapped in the vast, echoing museum, running from room to room, unable to find a way out.

But again that was ridiculous. She was letting her nerves get the better of her. There were exit signs everywhere and dozens of guards in the Hermitage, and the hotel was only five minutes walk from the front door. Besides, even though it was nearly midnight the sun had only just set.

She took a deep breath and focused. The Leonardo da Vinci Room was in the middle section of the wing overlooking the river. Along the way she surprised a dozing guard. He loomed out of the shadows, frightening her half to death, but didn't challenge her explanation that she'd forgotten something in one of the galleries. Gabbling something in Russian, he let her go.

The moment she was out of view, Laura started to run. It couldn't wait any longer. She had to know if she was right or wrong.

The door of the Leonardo Room was shut. She opened it cautiously and slipped inside. The gallery, illuminated by the street and city lights outside, had been restored to its usual immaculate state. By the look of things, every painting was back where it belonged – except the 'Benois Madonna'.

For a moment, Laura's heart seemed to stop entirely.

The masterpiece was gone. She stared around wildly. Perhaps it had been moved. Perhaps the museum curator had failed to realise that the original was the original and was even now trying to give it to Ricardo, thinking that it was his copy. The artist would explain that it wasn't and all would be well.

She sucked in a breath. There had to be an innocent explanation. If the painting had been stolen, surely the alarm would have gone off? If someone had pulled off a real life art heist in one of the greatest museums on earth, surely somebody, somewhere, would have noticed?

Tariq's phone beeped. The signal was back. She glanced down at it. There was another missed call from the unknown number. She clicked the search button again and the Internet symbol swirled. In answer to her question, the Wikipedia page for Deputy Prime Minister Ed Lucas uploaded. She clicked on the link and his biography unfurled, including the information she was looking for: his full name. Edward Ambrose Lucas.

It didn't really help. Lots of people had names beginning with A.

She continued reading. Under the section entitled Early Life, it detailed how Ed Lucas had been given up for adoption by his mother when he was just six months old and had been brought up by the Lucas family, who changed his first and last names, allowing him to keep only his middle name. They thought it might give him a fresh start. The name on his birth certificate was Anthony Ambrose Allington.

Anthony Ambrose Allington. Straight As.

There was a soft noise behind her. She turned in slow motion, the phone falling from her nerveless fingers. It hit the floor with a clatter.

'Good evening, Laura.'

'It's evening, but I wouldn't describe it as a good one. Hello, Mr A.'

18

ED LUCAS GAVE a mirthless laugh that sent chills through her. 'What I like most about you, Laura Marlin, is that you never disappoint me.'

He glanced into the shadows and Laura saw that he had an accomplice – one of his bodyguards. 'Didn't I tell you, Slither, that if anyone could crack our meticulously planned operation and ruin nearly two years of work, it would be this slip of a girl?'

'Yes, sir, boss, you did.'

'Against the advice of Slither here, and even against my own judgement, we waited for you, Laura Marlin. I was sure you'd come. Do you know that over the past few months, as you and your little friend and your meddling uncle have cost the Straight As tens of millions, the thing that has kept me sane is the notion that the best and most worthy adversary I've ever encountered is an eleven-year-old orphan? There's something almost poetic about it. I can't tell you how much I've looked forward to meeting you.'

Laura was so weak with terror she could barely stand, but she knew that her only hope of survival was to stay cool and play for time in the hope that a guard would burst in and rescue her. 'Well, it isn't mutual,' she snapped.

'Really? You strike me as one of the most honest girls who's ever breathed – as honest as Calvin Redfern, and that's saying something – but I don't believe you. All good detectives are infinitely interested in the workings of the criminal mind. Tell me that you're not at least a little bit curious about how we pulled this off?'

'I do have one question.'

'Fire away. Don't worry, we have two guards in our pay keeping an eye on things. No one will disturb us. Besides, the museum director was quite happy for me to have some private time up here.'

Laura's heart sank at the news that no one would be bursting in, but she did her best not to show it. 'Which came first – were you planning to steal the painting and the movie happened by coincidence, or did you happen to hear that there was a film being made about an art theft?'

'The film. About six months ago, a Hollywood business associate of mine heard about *The Aristocratic Thief* on the grapevine. He mentioned it to me because he found the story amusing and thought that we could do something along the same lines ourselves, only in real life. I suggested we go one step further and buy the film studio, Tiger Pictures. That would allow us to use the film shoot as a way of controlling access to the museum and, crucially, getting the alarm turned off.

'In the end it was easy. We bankrupted Tiger Productions, stepped in as fairy godfathers willing to finance both the company and their new movie, and the rest will soon be history.'

Laura did not bother to hide her disgust. 'I take it that Igor was your inside man.'

'He was. To me, it's important to have a sense of humour in crime, and we have had many laughs about Igor. As you can imagine, Igor is not his real name. In the Straight As, he is known as the Warrior – with good reason. He is a legendary kung fu fighter and a supreme athlete, who also happens to be rather good at acting. In real life, he is not yet thirty so the poor man had to endure an entire year of putting prosthetics – a false nose and wrinkled skin – on his face every single day. He was a good sport about it, figured it was worth it for his five million dollar cut.'

'Did he abseil from the window the way the thief does in the movie?'

'Nothing so dramatic. He simply walked unchallenged out of the gallery with Leonardo's "Benois Madonna" in a poster roll under his coat. We dismantled the frame and he tucked that into a box under his arm, along with a few Egyptian and Oriental antiquities. They'll keep the wolf from the door when we reach our destination.'

As he talked, Laura tried to sneak covert glances around the gallery. There had to be a way to attract attention or escape. She just had to keep him distracted. 'How did you swap the paintings before the shoot?'

'Ah, an unexpected lapse from Britain's youngest detective. You surprise me, Laura Marlin. We knew that once we'd got the paintings side by side, exchanging them in front of all those pampered dolts at the reception would be like taking candy from a baby. It was you I was worried about. I was convinced you'd work it out.'

'I did, but not in time. Let me guess. William Raven is an associate of yours or maybe just a man who owes you a favour. He's also an ex-conjurer. He exchanged the paintings while the waiter created a diversion with the spilled caviar.'

'Correct. He's no art thief, William, but he is a man who owes me a favour or two and he is, as you know, a gifted magician. At first he was reluctant to help and had to be reminded by my best men that he's benefitted quite considerably from my generosity and connections over the years. When we offered the additional carrot of a starring role in the film, he saw reason. When one has an ego the size of William's, fame is always going to be seductive.'

Laura glared at him. 'You're never going to get away with this, you know. Once he finds out who you are, my uncle will hunt you to the ends of the earth.'

Ed Lucas chuckled. 'Oh please. The funniest part of this whole Russia trip has been having Calvin Redfern, my nemesis, in charge of my security. A couple of months back, we planted a seed or two at MI5 about the Russian mafia having plans to assassinate me. It's been hilarious watching your uncle run himself ragged over the past week trying to protect me. As we speak, he is probably hard at work on plotting my safe return to London tomorrow. Another pointless exercise.'

'You're not going back?'

'Right again. Which brings me to the urgent matter of our departure. Slither, how are things looking on our exit route?'

A white light flared and Laura saw that Slither, who had greasily gelled hair and reminded her of Dracula, was holding a mini iPad. It showed the museum CCTV on a series of black and white screens.

'The passage is clear now. We should go, boss.'

'Agreed. A brief word of advice, Laura. A busy mind like yours will be considering all options for escape. Trust me when I say that it's not a good idea. If you scream, or set off an alarm, or look anything other than happy and placid if we have the ill-fortune to pass anyone on the way out, I have men in place poised to eliminate your uncle and your little boyfriend before you have time to blink. Am I making myself clear?'

Ed Lucas' strange electricity enveloped Laura so effectively that she felt powerless to struggle. Every hair on her body stood on end. But she knew his magnetism now for what it was: pure evil. She also knew that her chances of getting away from the Straight As would shrink to zero if they managed to get her out of the Hermitage unseen.

Slither grabbed her arm. 'Come on, little Miss Sunshine.

There's no time to waste. We're running late, thanks to you.'

'Wait!' cried Laura, forgetting to lower her voice.

The Deputy PM gave her a dangerous stare. 'I thought we had an agreement.'

'We did. We do. But where are you taking me? Can't you tell me that?'

He didn't answer, but he did nod to Slither, who let go of her arm. They walked on either side of her and slightly behind her, propelling her forward. Within seconds they were out of the gallery and moving silently down an emergency staircase. At the bottom, a guard saluted and unlocked a door. On the other side was a dark tunnel and the stench of damp and rotting fish.

The bodyguard turned on a torch and gave Laura a shove that almost sent her sprawling.

'Play nice, Slither,' warned Ed Lucas.

Disoriented, Laura tried to work out which way they were going. Were they heading towards Palace Square or the river? Judging by the smell, it was the latter. She didn't have to wait long to find out. As they rounded a bend, a powerful figure in black was removing a heavy iron grille.

'Recognise him?' Ed Lucas asked.

'No, but I'm guessing it's Igor.'

The Warrior's rough hands reached into the darkness and plucked her from the storm drain, as if she weighed less than the painting he carried in the cardboard roll beneath his coat.

They were on a jetty beside the river, screened by the riverbank from the nearby road. The black water gleamed like oil. A speedboat was tied to the dock, but nobody made a move towards it.

Laura felt nauseous with dread. 'Where are we going? Why are you doing this to me? If you let me go, I'll try to persuade my uncle to treat you leniently. I'll say that you can't be totally wicked if you were prepared to release me.'

Ed Lucas sighed. 'Laura, we've already been through this. You're coming with us and that's all there is to it. Don't worry, you'll enjoy it. It'll be a huge adventure and you do love adventures. In moments, we'll be on our way to a friendly South American country. We're retiring, you see. The Straight As, I mean. I have a theory that it's good to quit while you're ahead. Besides, the British Government might take a dim view of tonight's activities.'

There was a humming sound and the water in front of Laura began to churn as if a monster was rising from the deep. The speedboat bounced on the waves. Laura's hands, tucked deep in her pockets, shook uncontrollably.

'As for you, Laura, you needn't be afraid. You're going to have a great life. Four of our men have brought their wives and children with them, so you'll have plenty of friends to play with. We've bought a ranch in the middle of nowhere. You'll be able to ride horses in the sunshine. Isn't that the sort of thing you like to do? And if we ever do decide to come out of retirement, we can run our plans by you and you can tell us if we've made any mistakes. However, that isn't why we're taking you with us.'

Slither laughed unpleasantly. 'No, it isn't. What this is really about is payback against your dear Uncle Calvin. We reckon that snatching his precious niece would cause him prolonged pain, whereas if we shoot him it would be over in seconds.'

Ed Lucas grinned. 'So you see, Laura Marlin, Mr Avery was wrong. While everybody loves a hero at the cinema, in reality the bad guys mostly win.'

'Aren't you forgetting something?' said Laura.

The Deputy Prime Minister frowned. 'What's that?'

'You haven't won yet.'

The black water churned and gurgled and the hum grew louder. The monster surfaced, gradually taking the shape of a submarine. It bumped gently against the jetty. There was a hiss of air and a door popped open.

Ed Lucas gestured gallantly towards the submarine. 'After you, Laura Marlin,' he said pleasantly.

~ 19 ~

SKYE SHREDDED THE final page of the *St Petersburg Times* and sat on his haunches to admire a job well done. It looked as if there'd been a snowstorm on the carpet of the hotel room – snow that featured advertisements and headlines and was also speckled with crumbs from a raid on the mini bar. In addition, there was a lace from Tariq's boots and some soft, but unpleasantly fragrant, powder the husky had found in the bathroom.

It had been fun but now, once again, he was bored.

Footsteps drummed a muffled rhythm in the corridor. Skye rushed to the door, hoping it was Laura, but they continued past without stopping. Whining, he returned to the snowdrift of newsprint and flopped down. It was most unlike his mistress to be gone so long. It made him anxious.

In another minute, he was up again. This time he tried clawing at the balcony doors with his good left paw. Nothing happened at first, but then he felt something give. He clawed harder. There was a click and night air full of exciting smells flooded into the room. Skye stepped out onto the balcony and put his nose through the railings. The street was a long way below and the canal too far to break his fall.

He was about to retreat when he spotted a ledge. If he squeezed through the gap between the wall and the railings, he could probably reach it. His ears pricked. If Laura wouldn't come home to him, he'd go to her. Without so much as a glance at the chaotic room he was leaving behind, he jumped.

Meanwhile, at the Hermitage, the movie and museum directors were having words. Brett Avery was begging for time for just one more take.

'One more measly take. It'll take twenty minutes, tops.'

'That's what you said an hour ago, Mr Avery. My staff are exhausted. Your staff are exhausted. You are not being fair.'

'*I'm* not being fair? It was *your* idiot employee who unplugged our power supply in the middle of the last scene. And before that, another numbskull . . .'

'This could take a while,' Kay whispered to Tariq. 'Why don't you go check on Laura? I'll be down as soon as I can. Believe me, I'm as eager to get to bed as I'm sure you both are. But don't worry, tomorrow we get to have a long lie-in.'

Tariq took the service lift down to the basement room. It was almost empty apart from a couple of make-up artists, two extras, the bored guard still keeping watch beside the painting, and the roadies whose job it was to move the heavy equipment cases.

Tariq felt the first flutter of unease.

'Has anyone seen Laura?'

'Haven't seen her for a while,' said Gloria. 'She was looking at the painting and then she went out. She's probably in the bathroom, hon. Help yourself to a hot chocolate.'

Tariq thanked her and sat down to wait. As the minutes ticked by, he grew increasingly anxious. It was possible that Laura had been offered a lift back to the hotel, but it wasn't remotely probable that she would have accepted it without telling Kay. But maybe she'd decided that she didn't want to see the shoot after all and had gone up the stairs just as he was coming down in the lift. Kay would tell her where he was. Any minute now, she'd walk through the door.

To distract himself, he went over to the corner, where the guard seemed to have momentarily lost interest in protecting Leonardo's painting. His eyes were shut. But as Tariq approached, he sprang to life and lifted the cloth before the boy said anything.

'Great piktcha. Your friend, she like very much.'

Tariq smiled. 'I'm sure she did.'

He studied the picture. Tariq had spent years working his fingers to the bone creating tapestries for slave-masters both in Bangladesh and Cornwall, but it had never lessened his love of art. When he looked at a picture he tried to imagine how the artist had mixed his colours or achieved particular effects.

Now, however, he saw something different. Something that made the blood run cold in his veins. He saw the tiny smear on the blue flower.

His heart started to pound. For a moment he wondered if he'd somehow misunderstood and that the guard was well aware that this was Ricardo's copy and not Leonardo's original, but if that was true he wouldn't be watching over it.

Luc tapped Tariq on the shoulder, almost giving him a heart attack.

'I hear you were looking for Laura. She told me to let you know that she was nipping upstairs to fetch something.'

'Did she say where?'

'No, but I'm sure she won't be long.'

Thanking him and the guard, Tariq smiled and made his way casually across the room and out into the corridor, which was crowded with equipment cases. The basement was chilly but he'd started to sweat. He knew his best friend almost better than he knew himself. If she'd examined the picture and realised it was a fake, she'd have gone directly to the Leonardo Room to check if the original was still there. If it wasn't then it had either been stolen or was about to be.

As he walked along the corridor, trying not to attract

undue attention, he nearly tripped over a flat case marked Joker Productions. He stopped a man wheeling a trolley-load of lighting gear.

'Excuse me, who or what is Joker Productions?'

The roadie snorted. 'You're an extra, aren't you? They're the people who pay your wages, kid.'

Tariq's head swam. 'But I thought . . . I thought the name of the film company was Tiger Pictures.'

'It is. But after Tiger went bankrupt, Joker Productions stepped in with bailout money and agreed to finance this movie. They're silent partners. Their role is to take care of the bills, but they're not supposed to interfere in the making of the film. They only had one condition – that Brett and Kay cast William Raven in the starring role.'

'Any idea why?'

The man glanced over his shoulder and lowered his voice. 'Friend of mine told me that William was – how should I put it? – *obligated* to one of the head honchos at Joker. That's how he got the gig. Anyway, what's it to you? Tiger, Joker, what difference does it make as long as we get paid, right?'

'Right.'

The blood in Tariq's ears was roaring like an approaching tsunami. It was so far-fetched that it had to be a coincidence. Tiger Pictures, a successful film company, goes bankrupt almost overnight. Joker Productions – a company named after the Straight As favourite calling card – steps in to finance *The Aristocratic Thief*, using the film's storyline of an art heist as a smokescreen to set up a real life theft. But what if it wasn't a coincidence? What if it was, in fact, a deadly game? And where was Laura?

But he was jumping the gun. The Leonardo painting might be hanging in its rightful place in the Leonardo Room and Laura might be sitting happily with Kay, waiting for him.

As the lift hoisted him up to the first floor, he thought how strange it was that everything and everyone was continuing as normal when some sixth sense told him his world and theirs was about to explode.

On the first floor, all was silent. Outside the windows it was finally dark and he could see the masts of the tall ship that had been turned into a restaurant on the far side of the river. He moved silently along the dimly lit corridors, hoping to pass by unseen but feeling watched by the statues and paintings that lined the walls.

Ahead of him, a door burst open. Two of Ed Lucas' bodyguards emerged looking worried. Since the Deputy Prime Minister had supposedly left the museum at least an hour earlier, Tariq was surprised to see them. A guard stepped from behind a pillar and went towards them. The three talked briefly and the bodyguards rushed away in a different direction. Tariq used the opportunity to bypass the guard and get to the Leonardo Room via a different door.

The first thing he saw as he entered the gallery was the blank space on the wall where the painting had hung. The second was something glinting on the floor. He hurried over and picked it up. It was the back of his mobile phone. He recognised it because he'd scratched his initials on the side of it in case it was ever stolen at school. There was no sign of the rest of it.

Fear paralysed Tariq. Whoever had taken the painting had taken Laura, he was absolutely certain of it. The thought that it might be the Straight As made him feel sick to his stomach. He loved Laura more than anything on earth. She was his best friend and the best person he'd ever known. If anything were to happen to her . . .

But no, it wouldn't. He wouldn't allow it. He had to get help.

He thought of the scene they'd filmed earlier that evening. In it, the boy had touched a painting in order to set off an alarm. Maybe he should do that. Maybe that would be the quickest way to get help.

He dashed over to a picture, but before he could touch it he was seized by powerful arms. A hand was clapped over his mouth.

'Don't make a sound, Tariq,' whispered Calvin Redfern. 'The last thing we want to do is set off any alarms. Laura's life may depend on it.'

TARIQ HAD NEVER been so relieved to see anyone in his life. 'Sir, somebody has kidnapped Laura. I think it's the Straight As. They've taken a Leonardo da Vinci painting too.'

Calvin Redfern looked exhausted. His suit was wrinkled from travelling, his hair was sticking up on end and he'd lost his tie. 'Tariq, listen to me carefully. Ed Lucas is the boss of the Straight As. He's the man I've been hunting for my entire career – the kingpin of their whole evil empire.'

'The Deputy PM of Britain is Mr A? Are you sure? Isn't that the most catastrophic intelligence failure in history?'

'It would be right up there, yes. It might bring down the

Government. I only wish I'd figured it out sooner. My first clue was when Laura told me that he asked you who was likely to win – the good guys or the bad guys. It's not the sort of thing a politician would say to a child and it made me suspicious that Mr Lucas was not merely corrupt but was involved in a criminal conspiracy.

'Things started to fall into place. I began to do some investigation into his connections, both here and in Russia. What I found horrified me. Then I thought about the subject of the film – how a masterpiece is stolen by an aristocrat. It struck me as the kind of audacious stunt the Straight A gang loves to pull. When the pieces finally clicked into place, it suddenly occurred to me that you and Laura would be in grave danger at the reception. I jumped in a car and raced straight to Heathrow airport. Along the way, I tried desperately to get a message to one of you, but Laura's phone was switched off, Kay wouldn't return my calls, and you weren't answering.

'I arrived in Moscow about an hour and a half ago, but the traffic getting to the Hermitage was a nightmare. Meantime, I'd told Lucas' bodyguards not to let him out of their sight for a second, although I didn't reveal my suspicion that the Deputy PM was Mr A, which was just as well because one of those agents has vanished. Unless he, too, has been kidnapped, I think we can safely assume that he's a member of the Straight As.'

'Laura was going to text you,' Tariq said urgently. 'Did she do that?'

'I had a text from her around forty minutes ago, using your phone, to say that the evening had gone without a hitch and she was looking forward to some sleep. That temporarily reassured me. But as I pulled up outside the museum in a taxi, Jason, one of our loyal agents, called to say Ed Lucas had given them the slip.'

The door at the far end of the gallery opened and one of Ed Lucas' former bodyguards came in. Tariq recognised him from the film set. 'Sir, we've had a sighting. We think they're headed for the river.'

'Great.' Calvin Redfern put a hand on the boy's shoulder. 'Tariq, you more than anyone know how violent and deadly the Straight As are. If we are to save Laura, my men and I need to do this alone. The best thing you can do to help is to return to the basement crew room and pretend that nothing is going on. If an alarm goes off and people start panicking, we'll have no chance of catching the Straight As.'

'But can't I come with you? She's my best friend. I can help. I won't be in the way, I promise.'

'Tariq, the only promise I want you to make is that you'll go directly to the basement. I don't want you being taken hostage too. I wish I could take you myself, but every second counts. Here, have my phone. In an emergency, call Jason's number. I've got to run. Remember, not a word to anyone.'

♠

Tariq made his way back through the silent galleries, taking a detour to avoid two whispering guards. He felt utterly miserable. Laura had been snatched by one of the most evil men alive and it was all his fault. If he'd stayed with her, if he hadn't insisted on seeing an extra few minutes of filming, he might have been able to save her. If something had happened to her, he'd never forgive himself.

The lift pinged open on the basement floor. The room where the crew had been was empty except for Gloria and one of the wardrobe girls, who were poring over a catalogue. The guard was slumped beside Ricardo's painting, bleary-eyed with tiredness, oblivious to the fact that the real masterpiece was long gone.

Gloria glanced up. 'Boy, are you in trouble. Have you seen Kay? She's hunting high and low for you and Laura. Thinks you've been kidnapped by the Russian mafia. I told her that she's been working in Hollywood for too long.'

Tariq attempted a smile. 'Sorry, we were held up. I'll try to find Kay now. If I miss her, tell her that we're fine and she shouldn't worry about a thing.'

He went out into the corridor and looked at the fire exit at the far end. The crew had used it as an access door for loading and unloading equipment, which meant that it was likely to open onto the road or the river. If he went outside and kept to the shadows, he might spot something useful.

He'd given Calvin Redfern his word that he'd return to the basement, but he hadn't said anything about staying there.

A minute later, Tariq was standing on the riverbank under a blue-black sky. On the other side of the Neva, platinum light rose like steam from the dark silhouette of the Peter and Paul Fortress.

He tried to put himself in the shoes of the Straight A gang. They were audacious. They prided themselves on being the most elite criminals on earth and loved to shock and awe people with their terrible deeds. He could imagine them delighting in the planning of a robbery where art imitated life. The clue to catching them lay in discovering where life had not imitated art.

Could they, for instance, have abseiled out of the window of the gallery? Possibly, because if anyone challenged them they could explain that they were filming *The Aristocratic Thief*. On the other hand, would they have risked being captured on CCTV or being spotted by a policeman?

Unlikely. That meant they must have used one or two insiders to exchange the paintings and carry the masterpiece out of the museum. Who would they have used? William Raven? No, too self-involved. Ana María Tyler? No, who would risk antagonising her mother. Jeffrey, the horrid production manager? No, too stupid. One of the crew? A member of the museum staff?

Oh, it was hopeless. It could have been anyone or everyone, and all the while the Straight As might be spiriting Laura further and further away.

Tariq was furious with himself. He wished he had a mind like Laura's, which seemed designed to solve mysteries. He was reasonably strong and brave, but not nearly as gifted as his best friend when it came to understanding the psychology of criminals.

Think. He had to think. If they had to get away in a hurry with the painting, which way would they go? Palace Square was too exposed and a car waiting even momentarily on the river road would be noticed. By boat then? But where would they moor it and how would they get to it? A tunnel? A storm drain? Where would those things come out?

He hurried along the riverbank. A thought came to him. Kay had mentioned that a submarine was being used in the shoot the next day. If the Straight As were behind the making of the film, they might have used Ed Lucas' political or mafia connections to organise a real submarine – not some old relic that had been hired purely for the film, but a sophisticated one that could whisk them away to Mexico or wherever criminals went to lie low these days.

Tariq began to run. Kay had said that the submarine was docked on the river outside the Hermitage. If it was still there, he must be very close to it. Now that he knew what he was looking for, he spotted it almost immediately. It was moored in the dense, deep dark beneath the bridge, its panther-like hull almost invisible.

Gradually, his eyes adjusted. Three or four figures were milling around it. As one moved forward, there was a shimmer of light. A fraction of a second later, the blackness obscured it, but it was long enough for Tariq to guess it was Laura's blonde hair. They were putting her on board. If the doors shut, she'd be gone for ever.

He sprinted for the bridge. With any luck, the Straight As would be so focused on their task they wouldn't look up. What he was going to do when he got there, he didn't know. All he cared about was getting to Laura before the submarine vanished below the waters, never to be seen again.

So intent was he on his mission that he never saw a

cloaked figure step from behind a bridge support until he slammed into him. For the second time that night, strong arms gripped him and a salty hand covered his mouth.

'You're too late, Tariq,' said William Raven. 'Regrettably, your courage won't help you this time. You're going to have to let her go.'

Tariq bit his palm so hard that the actor snatched it away with a curse, wiping away blood.

'And what about you? Are you only able to stand up and be a man when the camera is on you, is that it?' Tariq said furiously. 'Are you a coward in real life? Or is it the money? Are they giving you a cut of whatever they make on the painting? It was you who swapped the pictures, wasn't it? You used your conjuring skills.'

The faint glow of a far streetlamp revealed William's features. He looked tortured. 'I might be a coward, but if you knew Ambrose Lucas – that's his real name, you know – you wouldn't blame me. He's a monster. A truly evil man. The stories of what has become of people who've crossed him are legendary. I had no choice. I had to help him or finish up dead or in the Hollywood gutter, my career over.'

'So you did it for the glory,' Tariq said scathingly. 'And now you're going to stand here and allow them to kidnap Laura and do nothing to stop them. I don't care about the stupid painting. It may be a masterpiece but it's nothing compared to Laura's life. Well, I hope you enjoy winning an Oscar and smiling on the red carpet knowing that you've stood by and allowed her to be snatched from the people who love her. You're pathetic. Now will you let go of me? I'm going to try to help her. I have the guts to do it even if you don't.'

He wrenched from William's grasp, but the actor grabbed his arm before he could move away. 'Tariq, don't do it. They'll only kidnap or kill you and what use will you be to Laura then?'

'At least I'll have tried to save her – unlike you. When I stopped the runaway carriage and saved you a trip to the hospital or morgue, you said you owed me. You said you always paid your debts. I guess you lied about that as well.'

The actor's eyes, usually so cold, lit up with rage and emotion. 'No, I didn't. I meant every word and I'll prove it to you now. On one condition.'

'What's that?'

'That you allow me to do it on my own. I'll try to help Laura, but if you get into trouble I won't be able to save you both.'

Tariq stared at him. 'You're serious?'

'Deadly.'

'OK. But hurry.'

William started to move away, then stopped. 'I'm sorry, Tariq. It should never have come to this. For what it's worth, if I could go back in time and do things differently I would.'

Despite the circumstances, Tariq felt compassion for the man. 'Just do what you can to fix things, Mr Raven.'

William ran to the river's concrete edge and looked down. 'Ambrose!' he yelled. 'Ambrose, wait!'

Without waiting for a response, he ran down some narrow steps and jumped onto the wood. All Tariq saw was his black cloak billowing like a parachute, followed by the sound of him crash-landing on a wooden jetty.

Tariq lay flat on the cold concrete so he could see what was happening without being observed. William had fallen hard and appeared to have sprained an ankle. He was attempting to struggle to his knees. In the yellow light of the open submarine door, he looked grey with pain.

'Don't do this, Ambrose. Take your painting and go, but release the girl. Run away to South America or wherever it is you're heading. I wish you all the best. But leave Laura with me. I'll take care of her.'

Ed Lucas had Laura by the arm and was advancing on him with an expression that would have shocked to the core anyone who'd ever voted for him or been charmed by him. He radiated malevolence.

'You pitiful fool,' he said. 'I ought to cut you down right here just for using my name, but I have a better idea. I'll take you with us on our claustrophobic journey to the bottom of the ocean. We can see how you like it down there.'

Without looking round, he said, 'Slither, come and get this ungrateful waste of space.'

'Freeze!' yelled a voice. 'This is Chief Inspector Redfern. Drop your weapons and put your hands in the air.'

There was a loud hiss and the door of the submarine slammed shut, sealing the Deputy Prime Minister outside, along with Slither and Laura. The water boiled as the great vessel began to submerge.

Ed Lucas swore, but he didn't waste time trying to appeal to the other gang members to let him in. Using

Laura as a human shield, he drew a revolver. 'If anyone tries to stop me, I will kill her. And don't make the mistake of thinking I won't do it. She's quite something, your niece, ex-Chief Inspector Redfern. A better detective than you ever were. But she's also trouble with a capital T and enough's enough.'

In one fluid move, he was in the speedboat, pulling Laura after him. She stumbled and fell against the boards, but he hauled her upright so it was impossible to shoot him without hitting her.

'Slither, untie the boat,' ordered Ed Lucas. 'Good, now come and join us. Adios, Detective Inspector Redfern. See you in hell, William.'

The speedboat motor roared to life and it surged away from the dock. Spray cascaded over Calvin Redfern and the two agents as they ran down to the water's edge. On the dock, William Raven was in despair. Up on the bank, Tariq was frantic. 'Laura!' he yelled. 'Laura!'

The speedboat bucked on the waves generated by the submarine. It veered dangerously against the river wall. There was a joyous bark and Skye came flying out of the darkness.

'Skye!' screamed Laura. 'Help me.'

And the husky leapt.

~ 21 ~

LAURA MARLIN LAY on the warm rocks beside the ocean and gazed up at the sky. It was the vivid blue of a brand new car, as if it had been buffed and waxed and finished off with a sprinkling of glitter. It looked inviting, good enough to dive into.

'It's weird, isn't it?' she said.

'What's weird?' asked Tariq. He was stretched out on one side of her, watching the ocean, while Skye, his fur standing up in wet spikes, was on the other. The husky had his eye on the picnic they'd laid out beside the rock pool. There was Cornish cheese, home-baked bread, tapas from the Porthmeor Beach cafe and chocolate brownies baked for them by Rowenna. Naturally, there was also ginger beer.

'It's weird that it's only two weeks since I was almost abducted in a Russian submarine and yet it feels as if it's something that happened to someone else in another lifetime. It feels surreal, like a dream.'

'I know what you mean. It feels like a movie.'

'It's going to be a movie, only we won't be starring in it. Well, Skye will but we won't and boy am I glad about that.'

Tariq propped himself up on one elbow and gave her a sly grin. 'You mean you don't want to be a famous actress any more?'

Laura sat up and opened a bottle of ginger beer. 'Tariq, if I ever express any interest in being any kind of actress ever again, you have my full permission to beat me over the head with a large mallet.'

'Oh, I wouldn't do that. A pillow maybe, but not a mallet. Besides, I think most people agree you make a pretty good detective. I mean, if you can stop Mr A, you could probably stop anyone.'

'I didn't stop Mr A. It was a team effort. Skye stopped him when he jumped in the boat and savaged him and that revolting man, Slither. You stopped him by persuading William Raven to do the decent thing. William's intervention caused Ed Lucas to step out of the submarine and bring me with him, and Uncle Calvin and the agents were brilliant once Mr A and his crime buddy ended up floundering in the river.

'The Russians were fantastic too. Thanks to the lightning reaction of their navy, the submarine was intercepted before it left Russian waters. Mr A and the other Straight A members will be brought back to the UK to stand trial at some point, but not until they've spent a few years reflecting on their actions in some awful Russian prison. They're called Gulags apparently.'

Tariq laughed. 'No wonder Brett and Kay changed their minds and decided to make a documentary about the making of *The Aristocratic Thief* rather than continue with the film itself. Truth is definitely stranger than fiction.'

Laura took a swig of ginger beer and shielded her eyes from the sun. A seal was bobbing in the waves.

'I can't wait to see what they come up with. Kay says that they're going to recreate the submarine escape scene, as well as the part where you stopped the runaway carriage. She emailed earlier to ask if we wanted them to cast actors who look like us, but Uncle Calvin says that for security reasons they can't. So you'll probably end up being a cute blond boy and I'll have flaming red hair or something.'

'Presumably they're going to keep Skye as Skye?'

'They have to, I guess. He's unique. We'll be able to go to see him at the cinema and he'll get lots of glory, but nobody can ever know any of the things that happened to us. For the rest of our lives, we'll have to keep it a secret.'

'That's okay,' Tariq responded. 'I've decided I like being someone hardly anyone ever notices. It makes it easier to observe them. Besides, I know already that I want to work with animals when I grow up. I'd choose being an unknown vet over a famous actor any day of the week.'

'Good choice,' Laura said. 'Our neighbour, Mrs Crabtree, came round this morning and she put it best.

Her theory is that fame is like a bubble. It looks gorgeous on the outside, as if it's been painted with pretty colours, but when you pop it there's nothing there. She said that life, love and friendship are what matters, and that what you do is more important than what you show. My uncle agrees. He says everyone loves a hero.'

She lay back down again and tried not to smile, but every time she remembered leaning over the handcuffed, dripping, woebegone leader of the Straight As, Edward Ambrose Lucas, and telling him, 'This time the good guys won,' she wanted to laugh. Stretching out a hand, she rubbed Skye's downy soft ears.

Tariq poked her in the ribs. 'Laura Marlin, I know that look. What are you planning?'

'I'm thinking,' Laura said, 'that we have the whole summer ahead of us, like a blank page with nothing written on it. I'm thinking that anything might happen – and it probably will.'

If you enjoyed *Rendezvous in Russia,*
you'll love the other Laura Marlin Mysteries . . .

~ DEAD MAN'S COVE ~

~ KIDNAP IN THE CARIBBEAN ~

~ KENTUCKY THRILLER ~

And don't miss Lauren St John's
White Giraffe quartet . . .

THE WHITE GIRAFFE

*'For a split second their eyes locked, the small sad girl
and the slender young giraffe, then the sky went dark.
Martine pressed her face to the window desperate to see the
white giraffe again, but it was impossible.'*

DOLPHIN SONG

*'Through the wild waves came one hundred dolphins
. . . leaping, dancing, cavorting . . . their silvery arcs
against the midnight ocean and crescent-mooned sky
were breathtakingly beautiful . . .'*

THE LAST LEOPARD

*'With one bound, the leopard smashed Martine to the earth.
His great paws thudded against her chest, his claws pierced
her skin, and then she was on the ground winded, and
in pain . . . 'Please don't hurt me,' she whispered.
'All I want to do is help you.''*

THE ELEPHANT'S TALE

*'The elephant's whole body trembled: a tear rolled
down her face . . . Some sixth sense told Martine that the
elephant's heart was failing because it had been broken.
Her freedom and family had been stolen from her.
She had nothing left to live for.'*

THE ONE DOLLAR HORSE

Fifteen year old Casey Blue lives in East London's
grimmest tower block, but her dream is to win
the world's greatest Three Day Event:
the Badminton Horse Trials.

But when she rescues a starving, half-wild horse,
she becomes convinced that the impossible
can be made possible . . .

RACE THE WIND

When Casey Blue's victory at the Badminton
Horse Trials earns her and Storm an invitation
to the prestigious Kentucky Three Day Event,
it is a dream come true.

But that dream is about to turn into
a nightmare . . .

the
orion star

★ ★ ★